TODAY

Single Dads, book 2

RJ SCOTT

Love Lane Books

Copyright

Copyright ©2019 RJ Scott

Cover design by Meredith Russell

Edited by Sue Laybourn

Published by Love Lane Books Ltd

ISBN - 9781688180123

This literary work may not be reproduced or transmitted in any form or by any means, including electronic or photographic reproduction, in whole or in part, without express written permission. This book cannot be copied in any format, sold, or otherwise transferred from your computer to another through upload to a file sharing peer-to-peer program, for free or for a fee. Such action is illegal and in violation of Copyright Law.

All characters and events in this book are fictitious. Any resemblance to actual persons living or dead is strictly coincidental. All trademarks are the property of their respective owners.

Dedication

Always for my family

Today
RJ SCOTT

ONE

Eric
———

ASH CAUGHT my arm as we arrived at the arch, very close to where he and Sean were going to exchange vows. Leo and I had taken down the fences between the two backyards last week, and the decorators put flowers and balloons everywhere, turning the space into a riot of movement and color. It was easy to relax here, back in my own space, with the specter of fire staying in the hills.

"Can I ask you a favor?" Ash asked.

"Sure thing." I smiled at him and waited for the details. I was exhausted and on edge, but I would've done anything to make sure that his and Sean's wedding went off without a hitch. Ash turned to me a little and nodded at the assembled family and friends.

"Third row, dark-haired guy with two children. Can you keep an eye out for him?"

Third row. Dark hair. I scanned the guests, and finally, I spotted the man Ash was asking me about. Wow. He was a sight for smoke-sore eyes. Cute, smaller than me, and thus everything I didn't normally look for in a partner, but still, he was looking this way, and he was gorgeous. My libido perked up immediately despite me coming off a four-day rolling shift that had nearly sapped every bit of my energy. *Hello, sexy dude in the third row.*

Of course, it didn't matter whether or not I was attracted to him because all he'd see back was a giant of a man, and even if he was interested in a big old firefighter, it would've been because he liked to be manhandled or dominated, or anything else I didn't want. Scratch that, I loved to manhandle the men I was with, but only if they did it back, and I knew the guy was sitting down, but he wasn't big at all, and I'd intimidate him. Still, I could look out for him today if it was important to Ash.

"Easily," I agreed.

Ash gave me a wide smile. Sean was a lucky guy, he'd found the one man who made him happy, and today he was marrying him. Sixty or so people had gathered, waiting for Ash and Sean to tie the knot, and there was a gentle murmur of voices, and the occasional chime of cell phones, or the *click* of a camera shutter. All of our neighbors were attending as well, and that included Gina, but I had plans for how to avoid her, which mostly included me hiding in the bushes. I'd take the dark-haired guy with me, and I could sit and eat and not flirt with him. Best of both worlds, I could keep my eye on him at the same time as chilling out.

Someone tugged on my pants, and I glanced down to see Mia attempting to climb my leg. I crouched down to visit with the gorgeous little girl, so envious that Sean got to be a new daddy to this precious bundle of light and laughter.

"Hey, baby girl," I murmured.

"Nen," she burbled away and patted my chest, yanking on my tie and laughing at me. She wore a lacy pink dress, which was covered in tiny white daisies, and holding back her bangs was the prettiest little flower I'd ever seen. She had sweet baby curls, and I wanted to kiss her head and hold her for the entire ceremony. But it wasn't my job to do that, as Leo waded in and scooped her up. He'd been given Mia-duty, and that was because he hadn't just come from fighting a brush fire that had eaten fifty acres and was only sixty percent tamed. I knew Sean and Ash were giving me space just to be me, but I wished I had the responsibility for Mia-wrangling because then I could maybe stay awake and forget all my aches and pains.

At least I'd been given the job of watching out for the mysterious dark-haired guy with the children—that would keep me awake, alert, and busy enough, so people didn't ask me questions. I needed that right now.

"What are you staring at?" Leo asked as Mia wriggled.

"Guy in the third row from the back, dark hair, cute," I said in a low voice.

He tracked where I'd been staring, but Mia tugged at him, and I doubt he got a perfect look. "Oh nice," Leo said, and I swear the asshole licked his lips and narrowed his eyes.

"I saw him first."

"Eric, he's so not your type," Leo summarized and winked at me. "Do I need to remind you about the Walmart incident?"

"No, you don't," I gritted my teeth, waiting for the usual teasing, and hoping that the wedding started soon.

Attraction hit me at the worst of times and with the poorest potential partners. Case in point, the unfortunate Walmart yogurt aisle incident that Leo was referencing. A happening that I wished I'd never shared with Leo and Sean, and which I would've liked to forget.

In my CALFIRE shirt, and reeking of smoke, I was so clearly a firefighter, and this smaller guy had swooned. Well, that was what Leo called it. All I know is small cute guy said he'd felt woozy and wanted me to carry him out of the store.

I'd held him still as he'd swayed, after all I *was* a trained professional, and the guy *had* been about to keel over. But, when he'd gotten close and suggested I pin him down, then fuck him in my car using cherry yogurt as lube, I'd declined.

Call me old-fashioned, but sex outside Walmart was a big no. Anyway, car sex was awkward at the best of times, add the fact I was six-foot-five, and the logistics of him and me, even with yogurt, were never going to work. Not to mention he'd wanted me to be a big, bad firefighter rescuing him from the graphic dangers of the dairy aisle. I'd turned him down, but had made the unfortunate choice of telling Leo, who'd told Sean. Friends. Who needs 'em.

I attracted needy men, it was a given, but it wasn't me who'd noticed that fact. Nope, that was Leo way back when we'd first met. I was already taller than everyone else, even that young, and stronger, and just, more. He'd noticed people were always asking for my help, and expecting me to be the strong one. I'd never thought about it, but yeah, I guessed I was. Not to mention the whole rainbow spectrum definition of bear that follows me everywhere.

So, back to cute and sexy, I knew there was no way I'd get a taste of Ash's friend. Either he'd be scared of me, or he'd want me to be his daddy, or something equally important to him that I couldn't deliver.

Still, it didn't stop me looking and thinking that spending some time in his company was a desirable proposition just for today. Because I was exhausted, and he was cute wrapped in a ribbon, or a suit, or whatever.

"Who is it anyway?" Leo asked as he rearranged one of Mia's errant curls that had escaped the tiny flower.

I don't think Ash had told me, but it was pretty easy to put two and two together. Ash had been anxious all week about a guy visiting from upstate who was super nervous and might not even come to the wedding. Brody, or Buddy, or something. Wait. Brady. That was his name.

"Brady, Ash's online friend."

"Do you think he likes cherry yogurt?"

I didn't get a chance to shove Leo, or give a witty comeback because first of all he was holding Mia, and also the music changed to some country song that had been Sean's choice, segueing into a piece of classical music that flowed around the gardens, and everyone fell silent. The officiant, a young woman with scarlet hair, gestured to us all, and we took our places.

"Today is a very special day," she began.

Ash and Sean couldn't stop smiling, even though their eyes were bright with emotion as they exchanged vows.

"You and Mia are my everything," Sean murmured.

"You make us a family," Ash responded.

I smiled. I didn't stop until my best friend and his partner were married, and seeing the affirmation of their love made everything in my life make sense. When they kissed, I was choked with emotion.

The officiant was right—today was very special.

TWO

Brady
———

TODAY WAS HARD.

I find social situations difficult, and the diagnosis of Developmental Coordination Disorder—DCD—that ruled my life made everything laborious and sometimes akin to torture. The sun is too bright, other people too close, and if it weren't for the fact I had Maddie and Lucas either side of me I would have run away faster than you could say "It's a wedding". I was sensitive to chaos, and the laughter and talking of the people around me was grating on me to the point I wanted to leave. I wouldn't though; the kids deserved me to be strong for them right now.

"Are you okay?" Maddie touched my arm, and I placed a hand over hers, smiling at her.

"Of course, sweetheart," I lied.

She snuggled in next to me, and I kissed the top of her head to let her know just how much I loved her, and how much her support meant to me. Even though she was only ten, she'd grown up with her clumsy uncle and his issues, and the amount of empathy she had was off the charts.

Lucas was just as careful with me, but he'd shown his concern in finding us chairs in the shade, and now he was on his phone.

Today is a good day. I will have fun.

I will not give in to anxiety, I won't be clumsy, or rude, even if the stress is already building. I will concentrate on the here and now and not run.

This was a special day, and I wanted to be present and focused on Ash and Sean's love story, which in my head was the stuff of Hallmark movies. Take one single dad Ash, falling in love with his neighbor Sean, a hot and sexy emergency room doctor, add in a tiny baby daughter, Mia, and it was a fairy tale I wanted to paint. I loved their journey up until today, and had discussed every little part of it online with Ash over the last year—everything from his falling for Sean, right up to why the hell it was essential to choose the right kind of flowers. I'd even hand-painted art for the cake itself, but even knowing I would be part of the fabric of a great love story, did I really have to come to the wedding?

I craned my neck to get my first proper look at real-life Ash. His online avatar for the forum was a grinning monkey holding a beer, but I'd seen actual real-life photos of him—some he'd shared with me, some on his Instagram which I'd located soon after we first connected. I wasn't stalking him, but he had such a nice way of writing, and he loved his daughter, and then he loved Sean, and I wanted to see the man who I'd connected with for real.

In return he'd seen two photos of me—each staged, neither of which would ever appear on a public forum like Instagram. Other than the single dads' forum I belonged to,

I didn't have much of a social media presence, and it was by chance that I was even on that forum. My best friend, Spencer, had been the one who'd signed me up over my protestations that I wasn't officially a dad. He'd told me I was fucking stupid even to think that way, but then Spencer never held back on anything. Maybe that is what happens in friendships, but he was my best friend as well as being my only friend, unless you counted Ben the delivery guy with whom I chatted on occasion.

I liked it that way. Isolation meant I wasn't going to make a fool of myself, and I'd met Spencer in grief counseling back when I was reeling from my sister's death, and my whole life had changed.

It had been Spencer who had encouraged me to write an answer for the next post on the forum. He'd also been the one to spell-check everything and had rewritten parts of it as I explained what I wanted to say. Fate had brought me into Ash's life and Spencer didn't fail to keep reminding me.

"You have to go to the wedding; you'll kick yourself if you don't." That is what Spencer had told me as late as last night when I'd still been considering not coming at all. I was glad I did but I was also terrified. I'd tried my hardest to get down to visit Ash before today, at least I told myself I'd tried my hardest, but Spencer calling me on my shit made me see I wasn't trying at all. He kept reminding me I was no more than thirty miles up the coast from Ash, but in the long year just gone I'd never managed it once.

"Is that him?" Maddie asked.

"Yeah."

Ash. Standing no more than ten feet from me.

I saw him before he saw me, but that was a given because he had so many guests there, and I was just one person among them, tucked away in the shade of the canopy. He was just as I expected him to be, smiling, and so damn happy, and the urge to go over and hug him and wish him all the best for the rest of his life was intense. Of course, I didn't because no one else here did anything dorky like rushing one of the grooms.

He caught my eye finally and smiled, and I sketched a wave at him, dropping my hand and smacking myself on my thigh. I didn't want to come off seeming like an idiot if he'd actually been waving at someone behind me. Ash was distracted by another man carrying Mia to the front of the guests, and there was an older lady who I assumed was Ash's mom, the one who'd been so hard on Ash before they'd reconciled. I knew for a fact that Ash still had some trouble with his past and what had happened with her, but he seemed to mellow more with each conversation we had about the situation. Maybe that was what falling in love did.

"I think my tummy hurts," Maddie said, and leaned on me.

All the worst-case scenarios hit me at once, and I went into super-protection mode. "Where, sweetheart?"

She pressed a hand to her belly, but not to where her appendix was, and she didn't appear pale or clammy.

"You only *think* it hurts? How bad is it?"

She snuggled closer. "Not that bad. I'm hungry is all."

I dug out a breakfast bar and handed it to her, and she nibbled on it as I tried to calm the hell down by cataloging each moment of the event in my mind, from the people to the color of the sky, and the blooms that decorated the arch. So many happy people, so many smiles, and part of me was genuinely excited to be there; it was just way down with the fear that I was trying to suppress.

I'd almost talked myself down from my stress when I saw *him.*

And *he* was staring right at me.

"It's hot." Maddie sighed dramatically. "Will it be cooler soon?" I couldn't answer her, too engrossed in checking out the man standing next to Ash, The man who stared right at me, nodding at something Ash was saying to him. I stopped myself from checking behind because that would be even more embarrassing. Was he smiling at me? I couldn't look away, and when he smiled, I felt some seismic shift inside me. What the hell? I'd never seen someone and experienced such a jolt of lust.

I don't do *lust.* Lust is messy and disorganized, and the opposite of what I need with my DCD.

But I couldn't rip my gaze away from the broad-shouldered, muscled bear of a man who was watching me, and it was only when Maddie repeated her question with an added force that I snapped the connection of our locked gazes. By the time I glanced back, Ash's husband-to-be had arrived on the scene, and the giant who'd caught my eye had his back to me.

He was wearing a suit jacket, and it pulled over his broad shoulders as he crouched down and disappeared from view. I don't know why he crouched, but I wished to hell he'd stand up. If only so I could have a better look at his firm ass and the thick thighs barely contained in the navy material.

"Eric," I murmured. This had to be Eric, the one that Ash had spoken about, the big man with the generous heart, the firefighter.

It *must* be Eric, although I glanced around for any other guys who were six-and-a-half feet, but no one fit the description. He was impressive, solid, and I knew from Ash that he was bi.

I had a chance with him.

That is, if he was into clumsy men with a head full of squirrelly, messy noise. "Idiot," I chastised myself softly.

"How long will we need to be here, Brady," Maddie asked. I hated it when they called me Brady. I wasn't their dad, I get that, but I was still their uncle. She used to call me Second Dad, but it didn't last long, only until she was about seven or so and came back from school in tears because, according to her friends, there was no such thing as a Second Dad.

It wasn't just Maddie that cried, but I saved my tears for after Lucas and her had gone to bed.

"Uncle Brady," I corrected gently, a little worried for a moment that she would get upset at being corrected.

"Sorry, Uncle Brady," she murmured instead.

"It's okay. I don't know how long this is supposed to last," I answered her question. I wriggled in my chair which was way too close to the row in front—I'd already imagined falling out of mine and ending up like a turtle on the immaculate lawn. The thick air made breathing difficult, the sun hot even in the shade, and my collar was too tight, and a man had stared at me and smiled.

Lucas' phone let out a sequence of obnoxious beeps.

"Please put the phone away, Lucas," I murmured.

He side-eyed me. "Nothing is happening here yet," his tone held an implied *duh,* but that wasn't new. He was twelve, and everything I did or said now had a *duh* thrown back in response. As much as I loved him, his attitude to life, in general, had taken a nosedive recently.

"Lucas—"

"I won't be long, promise; it's just this level."

I should've been responsible and made him pocket the phone, but if I did force him to cut his screen time short then he'd shove back with his nearly-teenage defensiveness, I'd get flustered, and the fragile peace I was holding onto would be gone.

Alternating between anticipation and terror was not a good headspace for me, and ever since Ash had invited me to attend his wedding that was exactly where I'd been. I was having a hard enough time even sitting still, let alone dealing with Lucas and me falling out and causing a scene. I couldn't go to a grocery store without flashbacks of temper tantrums from six-year-old Lucas, and the thought of anything like that here in the middle of a beautiful wedding was enough to have me sitting on my hands.

No one said that being sort-of-dad to Lucas and Maddie would be easy.

Today was hard. And tomorrow?

I couldn't even think about tomorrow.

"It's a beautiful day, and you're missing it," I encouraged Lucas with positive observation and reinforcement, as my therapist had said. I wasn't lying— today was a perfect San Diego day, with a cloudless cerulean sky, and the scent of flowers in the air. Even if it was too hot, too close, too everything.

"I'm nearly done," he said and hunched even farther over his cell phone which was still emitting beeping sounds that had to be annoying other guests who weren't there to get the second-hand experience of what he was playing. They were here for sunshine, love, and the happy couple. I glanced around to see if I could spot any other kids their age close by, just to check if I was overreacting. After all, according to Maddie and Lucas, there was no way I could get the new world, being how old I was. Twenty-eight wasn't old, and I knew that, but some days they made me feel ancient, or rather maybe I allowed them to make me feel that way.

That particular thought process worked out at two thousand dollars' worth of therapy.

"Why don't you give me the phone," I coaxed, loud enough that he would hear me, and hoped I wasn't so loud that I drew attention.

He turned sideways from me so that I couldn't reach it, and that was my answer.

"I think my phone is broken," Lucas tapped hard at the screen.

"What's wrong with it? Uhm… do you want me to look at it?"

Lucas shot me a glance of condescension, then sighed dramatically, "Yeah right." He pushed buttons and stared at the device as if that would help. Of course, it smarted that he wouldn't let me help, but that feeling didn't last long. After all, there wasn't any point in me looking at a broken phone at all. Lucas was stating the truth—I couldn't fix cell phones, I couldn't even use a phone like the one he had with all the complicated options. I still had my very first phone, which I'd learned to handle, but not anything newer and I could barely work my computer.

Problems? I had them. Buckets of them.

"Can I get a different water?" Maddie asked, and I picked up my survival bag, pulling out the water and handing it to her. "It's warm," she said and pulled a face that only a parent, or an uncle like me, would love.

Lucas twisted back. "Duh," he said in his best big brother tone. "That's because it's summer and it's hot." Then he rolled his eyes.

Maddie opened her mouth to snark back, but I sat forward in my chair to block them from talking to each other. At least Maddie was amenable for the most part. Lucas however, was the kid who would go out of his way to push the boundaries, but according to Paisley, my long-suffering therapist, defiance was healthy, and I should celebrate this fact.

Sometimes I thought my therapist talked shit. She was smart with her words and had a wall of certificates, but I swore she didn't have a single moment of experience with the mess and frustration of being a sort-of-dad who had to work way too hard at life.

I had to get Lucas to put the cell away because I'd already seen a few people turn. If any of them had talked to me and I'd had to have a grown-up conversation, I'd probably have grabbed the kids and made a run for it.

None of them smiled at me or told me it was okay. I bet they were all sitting there judging me, something I was well used to.

What did they want me to do? If I made a scene with Lucas, then things would get out of control, and everyone would see I had no power at all in our family dynamic. They'd know I wasn't a real dad.

One of them, a sharp-nosed woman in a violet hat, raised a single eyebrow which could have meant many things. I wanted to tell her that I'd never agreed to Lucas having a phone in the first place. It was his Grandpa Bob, his dad's dad, who'd given it to him. I knew he'd done it because he and the kids' Grandma Jessie were trying to outdo each other post-divorce, but he'd gone against my rules, and he'd done it on Christmas morning when I couldn't exactly say no. I suspected that this Christmas, Maddie would be getting her own phone as well, and then we'd have the same issue.

Lucas repeatedly hit one button, I assume in an effort to fix whatever the problem was. "Please, Lucas," I said, keeping my voice low.

"In a minute."

Those three words framed my entire parenting experience. Please, clean your room, *in a minute*, please, do your homework, *in a minute,* please, come and eat dinner, *in a minute.* The normality of it was reassuring, but on bad days it pushed my buttons.

That particular *minute* was magic to kids and could stretch anywhere from five to sixty, and sometimes it was easier to let things slide — anything for a quiet life.

"Who is this guy getting married again?"

I sighed internally but pasted a happy smile on my face when I spoke to him, attempting to silence potential complaints with positive goddamned energy and light. "You know who it is. It's my friend Ash."

"Wish they'd hurry up," he muttered next to me. "I

don't see why *we* had to come with you." He was just loud enough that I could hear, but I hoped to hell no one else could.

"Because I'm in charge and you're the child," I said instead, without opening my eyes, and thank the heavens, after a huff of displeasure he stopped talking.

He wasn't a nasty kid, neither was Maddie, and I loved them so much that it hurt. I would've done anything for either of them, and I hoped they never thought otherwise.

"Shhh," the woman in the hat hissed back at me.

I ignored her as best I could, pleased that Lucas was off the phone, and then my mind wandered back to Eric, and in my random way, I went from thinking about his job to the color of his hair. Right in the middle of all of that, I realized sex had happened in my head. I didn't mean I was having a waking wet dream or anything. I was lost in contemplating what it would be like to have someone as big as him hug me. Would he encompass me completely? Would he be able to pick me up? Crush me? I'm five-ten and top the scales at one-sixty-eight on a good day. So yeah, he could've probably surrounded me, been my protector, kept the rest of the world away. But then, what if he was just that, and wasn't interested in me calling any of the shots, what if he thought I was fragile, or damaged, or needed to be fixed.

I corralled my thoughts and concentrated on the service. It was brief and beautiful, and emotion choked me, with tears pricking at my eyes. Even the kids sat up to get a better look, but as soon as the ceremony was over, and the congratulations began, Lucas and Maddie were up off their seats and heading for the bushes at the end of the garden. They did this a lot, isolating themselves away from me, even if they did bicker when they were on their own. That should have been a good thing, I wanted the siblings to be close, only not to the detriment of our relationship. I didn't *want* to be frozen out.

I followed them to where they stood huddled next to a fence.

"There'll be food soon," I said, with above-average enthusiasm.

Lucas kicked at a bush, his expression mutinous. "We could have stayed over at Spencer's place," he said and kicked out again. This time a flurry of leaves fell from the California coffeeberry, and when Lucas made to kick it once more, I moved forward, but not soon enough, as the plant sagged pathetically. Poor thing, it had just been sitting there, growing, and now it was hurt.

"Lucas, come on," I pleaded.

I often thought back to the little kids who had become my responsibility, the cute four-year-old and his chubby toddler sister and wondered where I'd gone wrong. Not in general, but specifically. There had to have been a single moment where I'd fucked everything up, but I couldn't remember when it was.

"Uncle Brady, are you okay?" Maddie interrupted, and I turned my focus on her.

"Of course, why?"

"You look all…" She smoothed her palms on her face and grimaced briefly, which was the way she described me when I had a moment of panic. There was a hint of deviousness in her eyes, which belied her innocent expression, and all I could think was, when had the cute baby become someone who tried to manipulate me? Sorrow knifed me, that I even had some chink in my armor that she'd identified. A dad should've been stalwart, unflappable, a role model, not some weird, mismatched mess who couldn't get his head around something as ordinary as a freaking wedding. I stayed patient.

"I'm fine, Maddie."

"We can always go, Uncle Brady," Lucas added. "If you need to."

"We're not going," I thumbed over my shoulder, "there are loads of other children here, go and make some new friends."

"I don't need new friends," Lucas said, and his voice was louder now. "If you'd let me stay with Spencer, I could have been with Liam, and Liam is my friend."

"Lucas—"

"I could have stayed there as well," Maddie interrupted. It seemed she was getting good at that now.

I pressed fingers to my temples but dropped them. *Show no weakness.* "I'm sorry guys; I thought you'd enjoy it—"

"Well, we're not," Lucas finished, and crossed his arms over his chest.

"Nope, I wanna go home." Maddie copied his stance.

Lucas sniffed, "Yeah, this is stupid—"

"Whoa," a warning voice had me turning so fast I tripped over my own feet.

Someone gripped me, and I glanced up right into Eric's dark blue eyes. Up this close, he was just as intimidating, bigger than he'd seemed at first, his hair was short, and light brown with gray at the temples. I knew he was the same age as Ash, which put him just past thirty, but he was rocking the silver fox style. When he didn't say anything, I wondered what he wanted. Was he there to talk to us, or to explain that he was there to take all three of us off the property?

Instead, he released me and set me away, supporting me until I was steady, then turned to the kids. "There's food, guys," he thumbed over his shoulder. That wasn't going to work with them, I'd already mentioned food, and they'd dismissed it out of hand. Anyway, who did Eric think he was to interfere in our lives? It served him right if they shredded him alive, and I winced internally at the thought.

Whatever happened, however Maddie and Lucas reacted, all I knew was that I had a front-row seat to the carnage.

THREE

Eric

A PAIR OF CHILDREN, couldn't have been much more than ten or so, stared up at me. They stopped sniping at this Brady guy who Ash had asked me to watch, and instead, they stood, mouths open, and silent.

"Food," I repeated and thumbed at the tables that were laden with so much it was a wonder they stayed upright.

The girl, younger I think, with her long blonde hair in a complicated braid, blinked at me and sidled closer to the boy, who was taller and gripping a cell phone so hard I thought it might snap.

"Maddie, Lucas, why don't you go and get some food," Brady said, his voice soft, his tone fearful. "Please," he added.

They took a large, cautious circle to avoid me, then hurried over to the food, which meant I was alone with the cute brunet.

"Eric," I introduced myself and held out a hand. "I'm a friend of Sean's."

"Brady," he said, and we shook long enough to give

each other respect, and only until he pulled his hand free. "I know you're a friend, Ash told me, he's the other groom." His eyes widened as he spoke. "Of course, you know that. Anyway, he's told me a lot about you. I'm a friend too, well, sort of, I guess Sean doesn't know me very well, and Ash probably hasn't spoken about me."

Something about Brady seemed hopeful as his words spilled out, and concern twisted in my chest. I'd learned to read people in my job. The number of times we'd been called to a jumper, or to a person trapped in a fire, and knowing the micro-expressions on someone's face was sometimes the single clue that the person I was there to save was going to do something stupid. Brady had that look of bewilderment and fear in his eyes.

I felt pathetically protective all of a sudden. "He's told us a lot about you," I exaggerated. I didn't *see* a lot of Ash, and Sean had moved next door just before Christmas last year. But I knew enough to be convincing. "You're an artist, you care for your niece and nephew, and you and Ash met on a forum for single dads."

Brady was shocked, then smiled cautiously "And you're a firefighter with CALFIRE, you specialize in brush fires."

I nodded but didn't add anything else. Ash had asked me to keep an eye on Brady today, and I would do that, but it wasn't going to be done by talking about my job.

"I'm sorry about the fires," Brady said, and then rolled his eyes. "Not all of the fires, just the ones in Harvey. Not that all fires aren't bad, but the ones in… I'm stopping now."

"I get what you meant. Thank you, it's been tough.

Anyway. It was a lovely wedding," I changed the subject. The last thing I needed was to be dragged back into thoughts of what was happening sixty miles away from the whites and blues of this beautiful backyard wedding.

He nodded and gave me another smile. I fell into his hazel eyes, and I think I stayed there for way too long, hypothetically, because his smile faded, and I knew I was coming across as way too intense.

This called for another change in the subject.

"Beer?" I asked.

"Just water, please," he said.

I went to the table and grabbed a soda for myself and icy water for him, slipping back through the crowd, as much as a guy my size can slip, with the two drinks, and avoiding conversation with everyone. I was as sociable as the next guy, but right now I wanted to talk to Brady. Not just because Ash had asked me to, but because he was cute, and had a lovely smile, and seemed like he might need me.

Leo was right, people need me to help them, but it wasn't just that—I was hardwired to want to help people right back.

I handed him the bottle, and he reached for it, fumbling the hold and then gripping it as if he was going to drop it. I wished I could've had a beer, because even if it wasn't an option today, alcohol of any kind might have helped with the tension in our house this morning.

Sean had stayed over in his old room last night and had been a mess from the minute he'd woken up, stressed about everything being perfect. We'd all dropped the ball over the last few weeks, and I knew that was why he was frazzled. He hadn't even been home a lot this last week, working triage on the fires, volunteering even though it left him out of the loop at home. Not that Ash had seemed concerned, he'd had it all under control, and loved that his fiancé wanted to work with the CALFIRE teams up in the hills.

In fact Leo, Sean and I had all become involved in the fires above Harvey, and I still was, unofficially. Even though this day had been booked as vacation for months, I had my cell on me if anyone needed me. Hence no beers and my truck parked out on the road where it wouldn't get blocked in.

I pulled two chairs out and set them back by a coffeeberry bush, in the shade, and out of view of the gathering, all to get some peace before people saw me sitting there and wanted to know how I was, or how I was feeling, or how the Harvey fire was a tragedy. It was a tragedy, people had died, acres of brush burned, houses lost, but I refused to talk about it at Sean's wedding. Right up until yesterday, we'd thought we might lose a couple of ranches near Harvey, not to mention Harvey itself. I placed my soda on the chair and then thought about food.

"You hungry?" I asked Brady, and he shot a quick look at the chaos around the buffet table. I imagined him thinking he'd like something to eat, but that there was no way he'd get any right now. "Hang on," I said, and muscled my way politely to the back of one of the tables, plating up a variety of nibbles and returning to the seats. I avoided three questions about the fires, two about work in general, all replied with a simple "I'll come find you later", which was a blatant lie.

Brady stood where I'd left him, his knuckles white where he gripped the back of a chair, so I sat first, taking away the whole intimidation factor of being way taller than him, and holding out a plate of food.

"I didn't check if you have allergies, but everything is nut-free, apparently, and there are all kinds of alternatives like vegan and—"

"I don't have any allergies," he interrupted, and took the plate, holding it tight then carefully sitting on the chair before leaning a small distance from me. His body language screamed that he didn't want to be there, or this close or whatever, so I made a big show of shuffling my chair away and at an angle as if I needed to get comfortable. As soon as I moved away, he appeared to relax, and I felt as if I was the smartest person alive.

"Sean told me that you have two children, so I'm guessing they are yours?" I gestured to the two of them standing with some other kids, the whole group of them stuffing their faces with food.

"Yeah, Lucas and Maddie. But I guess you know I'm not a dad for real, they're my sister's children... were, I mean... still are..." He took a breath, and I watched him center himself. "I'm all they have, but they don't call me Dad."

"They live with you?"

"Oh, yes, of course."

"You feed them, clothe them, put bandages on their hurts, read them stories, listen to their fears?"

He blinked at me, "Uh-huh," he offered after that pause.

"So you're a dad then," I summarized.

"Uncle for sure."

"So you're *Uncle* Brady."

"Or just Brady," he shrugged as if that was no big deal.

I got the sense this was a no-discussion subject, so I went onto the next thing I knew about him. I didn't have a long list to work with, but I hoped that something resonated enough to get him to relax. Being as tired as I was, it was hard to concentrate on conversational topics, but one fact I had I thought might work.

"Ash told me that you're an artist, and you helped him with the cake design."

"I'm not an expert in cakes," he defended and tilted his chin, "but it turned out okay."

Did he imagine I was going to argue? He certainly appeared primed for me to criticize, but I wasn't going to at all. It was a stunning design.

"Only 'okay'? It's amazing. I love that at the front it's a standard cake, but around the back, it's got all those beautiful images of Sean, Ash, and Mia that you drew."

"Oh," he dipped his head shyly. "Thank you."

Still with the disbelief? Brady needed to see I was telling the truth, and I couldn't for the life of me understand why that was important to me. It just was.

"Oh yeah, I've never seen anything like it. Did you create the drawing on the icing itself, or whatever they used at the back there?"

"Yeah I did, it's a technique where I drew it on parchment paper first. Sean and Ash inspired me, they're so happy, and Mia is a beautiful baby, well, toddler now, I guess."

"Very much a toddler, did you see her walking?"

He glanced behind him as if he was expecting Mia to be there. "I'll probably see her later when it's all calmer."

"She's such a little spitfire, and Leo has been given his best friend mission today, he's on baby-duty." I held my breath as I considered what I'd said. Would shy Brady think that, as Sean's other best friend, I was on Brady-duty? Not that I was really, all Ash had said was to keep an eye on Brady, so I wasn't following him around or…

Yeah, I really was doing that very thing.

I'd gotten him a drink, fed him, and was now staying with him to look out for him. It wasn't arduous, Brady was seriously cute, with his soft brown hair and his thoughtful dark eyes, and the fact that he was shy, but didn't seem intimidated by me at all.

Maybe I was wrong. Perhaps he'd hold his own in bed.

Stop it. Now.

I shifted in my seat, my pants a little too tight at the image of shy Brady in my bed. Imagine what he'd be like once I had him on edge when I was—

Stop it, for fuck's sake.

"Are you okay?" Brady asked, cautiously.

"Sorry, I was miles away," I apologized. "So, uhm… tell me about Lucas and Maddie? How old are they?"

He smiled at me, "Lucas is twelve and Maddie, ten."

I recalled what I knew about Brady and the kids. Ash hadn't explained much past the fact that Brady was single, dad to two kids, and that he was an artist. Oh, and of course I'd just found out the children were his sister's kids, or had been, or whatever he'd tried explaining to me. Other than that, my internal file for the intriguing Brady was empty.

I waited for him to expand on the explanation, but the sliced chorizo he was poking at appeared to be taking his entire focus, so I changed the subject.

"What kind of artist are you?"

"All kinds," he said, and at least left the chorizo alone to look up at me. "Portraits from photos, web designs, logos, and some graphic art. I had a company once," he began, and then worried his lip and frowned. "Well, the start of a company, but I gave that up when I moved to my sister's house to look after Maddie and Lucas. I've drawn for some graphic novels."

"That's so cool, any I would have heard of?"

He gave me a soft smile. "Do you even read graphic novels?"

"I've seen some. Frankie, he's a colleague at the firehouse, he has an entire collection of them, and I've seen how colorful they are." Was it okay to say that? Had I just dissed an entire sub-genre of reading material with my naiveté?

He brightened. "The niche I draw for is alien romance, and it's an online LGBTQ graphic series called Mu 7, so I doubt you've seen any of my work."

He was right. I didn't have a lot of time to read, but through Frankie, I'd found *Yuri on Ice* which was a figure skating show online, not that I understood many of the terms that Frankie used to describe it. Anyway, I enjoyed the story; it was sexy, hot, cute, inspiring, and just what an overworked firefighter needed to take him right out of his head. Made all the better when Frankie had pretended to pirouette like the figure skater in the book, caught his foot on a break room chair and fell on his ass.

We sat in silence for a few moments, and I noticed how cautious Brady was at eating, how carefully he picked up the food with his fork, and how deliberate his actions were to get the food to his mouth. He was seriously nervous if he worried about spilling stuff on his shirt, although maybe it was an expensive shirt. Who knew?

"It was a lovely ceremony," I said after I'd polished off my entire plate. He stopped eating and smiled.

"Yeah, it was," then he sounded a little more wistful. "It must be so nice to find someone to love in this weird world of ours."

That statement sounded strange.

"Doesn't matter about the world," I began, "I honestly believe we all have the chance to find love somewhere. Don't you?" I didn't usually wax lyrical, but after the week I'd just had, today I was feeling mellow and happy for Ash, and I wanted everyone at the wedding to be happy. Even Leo's Aunt Bridgette with her godawful purple hat and her opinions on gay marriage had cracked at least one smile today.

Only Brady glanced away and didn't smile. Why was his answer so vital to me, and why did I want him to smile?

"Don't you think so?" I prompted.

FOUR

Brady
———

THE CHANCE TO find love anywhere? That was one hell of a profound statement that Eric had made.

"I guess so," I responded finally.

There were some things I understood about love, though. It was obvious that I had loved my parents, John and Louise, both gone from us now, Mom a long time before Nicole, Dad a few months after Nicole had died, passing away from what I thought of as a broken heart. Not even his son and grandchildren could hold him in this world, and with him gone, I'd genuinely been left alone, a scary thought even on a good day. They'd had me and my sister, Nicole, late in life, but they'd been the best kind of caring parents, and my sister and I had been happy kids in a loving family where affection was unguarded and offered freely.

I still loved Nicole. It didn't matter that she'd been gone eight years. When I thought I was forgetting what she looked like, or what a sibling's love could be like, I panicked and ended up standing for ages in front of the wall of photos in our hallway. But even when her features slipped from my thoughts, I still knew the love I had in my heart.

I'd known the best kind of love, and the worst of grief that came with it, a tidal wave of sorrow and heartache that had taught me that everything could be destroyed in one horrific moment.

I'd thought I loved my last boyfriend, but I hadn't really. Robert was just another in a long line of men I'd met who'd thought I was a good guy, but soon realized how broken I was, and just wanted to fix me. Robert went the same way as the others, vanishing when they realized that I put family first and that I didn't *want* or *need* to be fixed.

Then there was Maddie and Lucas, the children my sister and her husband Dan, had gifted to me. For the longest time after the accident, Dan had clung to life, and the children weren't mine to care for in a legal sense, although it was me who'd held them as they'd cried for their mom and dad. The three of us had been in limbo, and only when Dan had finally passed, had the full enormity of the kind of love I needed to have for them hit me hard.

I know you can love them as much as we do. That was what my sister and Dan had written in the letter with their will. They hadn't seen someone broken, or lacking in any way, they'd seen me as being able to care for their kids.

I wished I had their conviction.

Unconditional love, a powerful emotion that forgave tantrums, black marker pens on white T-shirts, spilled drinks and being told I was stupid. The last was hard to hear but still, if it was Lucas or Maddie who said the words, then I forgave them out of love.

"Depends on the kind of love," I added when he wouldn't stop staring at me. "I don't think I want anything like this." I waved a hand, and my plate slipped, but more by luck than judgment, I stopped everything slipping to the ground. Of course, my thumb ended up in the mayonnaise, but I sucked it off, and that was another crisis averted.

Eric let out a small noise, halfway between a squeak and a word, and I glanced at him to see what was wrong. He'd turned away from me though, and was staring out over the yard as if his life depended on it. Weird.

"Are you okay?" I tried for considerate.

He nodded before slowly turning back to face me. "Yep," he wriggled in his chair a little. "You wouldn't want to get married?" he took a long swallow of his soda.

"I'd have to get past the casual sex stage with the right man," I joked. Then I waited for him to agree with me, but yet again he looked anywhere but at me, and I don't know if I was reading him right, but he appeared preoccupied. Still, just because he was distracted, it didn't mean that he was bored sitting with me, it just meant that something else in his life was more of a priority at that moment. He could've been worried about the guests, or the food, or I don't know, fire safety or something.

It had taken years of therapy to get to the point of believing that not every stranger was pissed at me.

And at least I was there at the wedding interacting with people. In my way, I think I'd helped Ash in the run-up to creating this perfect day, but up until last night I hadn't even RSVP'd that the three of us were coming. He'd said he understood I must have had reasons, but he'd never once pushed. He knew about the dyslexia, but the other stuff? That wasn't a discussion I wanted to have. It wasn't that I didn't want him to know, it's that typing out the mess would take hours, and someone would have to check it for me before I pasted it.

I was desperate to change the subject, and picked the only thing I knew for sure would stop the focus being on me.

I knew that Eric, Leo, and Sean had been involved in working the forest fires on the mountain and that Eric would probably be exhausted today. I knew all that because Ash hadn't slept much last night, and we'd been talking until two a.m. about the fire staying up in the hills, and how it was contained enough to allow Eric to attend the wedding. I also knew Eric was part of a CALFIRE team that got called in with specialist equipment to fight the fires that seemingly ran year-round. Ash had told me Eric had been on duty for the equivalent of six shifts without much downtime because it was all hands on deck.

Together, we'd been watching the online Crisis Map which showed the spread of the Harvey fire. Authorities were closely monitoring public resources to keep people safe, secure, and prepared, and advice was that travel was okay. Sue me if a small part of me wanted to use fires as a reason not to leave my hometown. The same fire that Eric was assigned to, the same one that Leo was assisting at evac, and the one that Sean had volunteered at, backing up onsite medics. The fact that I'd even considered using something so dramatic and earth-destroying as an excuse to miss a freaking wedding made me feel small. People were out there fighting an all-consuming natural disaster, and I was stuck in my head scared to confront life.

Maybe that was what shook me enough to have made me come today? Who knew?

"I hear you were working on the forest fires," I wished I hadn't said anything like that when I saw his closed-off expression.

"Yeah, it's been a hard week, a hard season," he summarized. "Tell me more about your art."

Even I wasn't stupid enough to see he was changing the subject, so I pulled up facts about what I did, and almost had them all in order.

"Brady!" I tensed at the voice behind us, then half-turned in my chair and realized I couldn't avoid Ash, who was heading our way, with his husband in tow. They were stunning, both in dark suits, the only difference between them the blue shade of their ties. I recall that online discussion about exactly how many shades of blue there were. I knew for instance that Sean's tie was steel-blue and Ash had gone for baby-blue. Ash dropped Sean's hand and opened his arms wide, and I knew I should get up and walk into a hug. I wanted to. Hell, I'd practiced this moment a hundred times in the mirror at home, but not ever with a plate of food on my lap, which meant said plate ended up in the grass upside down, the chair toppled backward, and me falling over my own feet.

Ash caught me and pulled me close, and I hugged him, attempting to ignore the embarrassment of how much I'd messed up just standing.

He'll say something about what happened. He'll laugh. Maybe he'll get impatient.

"I'm so happy to meet you for real finally," he said instead, and tugged Sean forward. "This is Sean."

I offered a hand to Sean, but he ignored it and hugged me instead. "Thank you for the cake design; it's stunning," he stepped away.

I didn't know what to say. In that awful moment, I was speechless because my tongue felt too big in my mouth, and my brain failed to provide me with any backup.

"We have to meet up, after we get back from the honeymoon," Ash said, before I could come out with anything resembling words.

"I'd love to," I lied, and tried my best to make it look as if I was incredibly excited to meet Ash again.

"And thank you for the help with the honeymoon," Ash added.

"You're welcome."

They were going to South Carolina. I'd helped Ash pick the hotel, with just the right levels of luxury, perfect sandy beaches, the right temperatures during the day, and had researched to make sure it was rainbow, and child-friendly as they were taking Mia. I'd like to go there myself one day.

"Are you having fun?" Ash asked.

"I am, and it was a beautiful ceremony."

Sean hugged Ash close and pressed a kiss to the top of his head. "Ash has been so excited to meet you," he said

"Ash?" a woman's voice broke into our chat, and I was grateful I didn't have to find conversation. Ash's mom headed our way. "They're saying twenty minutes for cake and speeches."

"Mom, this is my friend, Brady."

I shook hands with her when all I wanted to do was ignore her hand because of the way she'd been with Ash when he'd come out as gay. The day I'd come out as gay to my mom she'd hugged me, then sat me down to explain how I needed to be careful because adding another social pressure to my life was a heavy weight. Even so, she'd listened and loved me, and had never tried to change me. To be fair to Dad, when I'd told him he'd taken it well, but then pretended it wasn't a real thing, and I'd never shoved a relationship in their faces.

Of course, I'd have to have had relationships in the first place to be able to do that. The last one had been Robert, and he hadn't lasted that long. Not that I'd wanted him to, after all, he was an asshole who'd pitied me and made me feel even more stupid.

Stop thinking about Robert.

"Nice to meet you," she said as we shook, and she smiled the prettiest smile, one that was eerily similar to Ash's.

"And you."

"We have to keep mingling, and then cake!" Sean exclaimed hugged Ash tight. "Cake!" he repeated.

Ash laughed, "I swear my husband is more excited about the cake than the honeymoon."

Sean didn't let him go and then kissed him hard. Right in front of us.

"What was that for?" Ash asked when they separated, as he placed fingers to his lips and had this dazed expression on his face.

"You called me your husband," Sean murmured, and they kissed briefly again. I couldn't stop watching, not only because they were right in front of me, but because they had everything I wanted.

Not a wedding.

Not being married.

It was more straightforward than that. I wanted someone who kissed me as Sean had just kissed Ash.

Sean and Ash gave me one last hug, but as soon as they left, I headed away from Eric, because the need in me was raw, and I could feel confusion and desire warring in my clumsy-ass body, and I needed to find a quiet space for a moment. I felt sick, and my head was spinning.

"Wait," Eric called after me, "are you okay? Can I get you another drink?"

I stopped and turned slowly, so I didn't end up on my ass. "I'm not thirsty," I said, but he came toward me, reaching out and touching my shoulder.

Why are you touching me as if I'm something precious?

"Is everything okay?" he asked me, and there was an excess of compassion written into his expression and in his body language.

Oh yeah, everything is fine. This sexy man had his hands on me, and just his touch had me wishing we weren't in a garden full of people.

"I'm good," I said.

We stared at each other until he cradled my face. His hands were warm, and I wanted to bury myself in his arms and never move. I could see the spark of something in his eyes, the connection that meant we had a mutual attraction. When he didn't immediately remove his hand, I took the initiative by pressing my cheek against his palm. In my head, the action was tiny and subtle, and I couldn't fail to hear the soft groan he let out. He leaned closer, and I thought he might kiss me.

"Brady," he said low and urgent. "I want to keep talking to you."

I saw his eyes close up, how red they were, from smoke and lack of sleep, I assumed. He wasn't thinking straight. Anyway, what did I have to say to him?

"I have to find the kids," I said, leaving and not looking back. Eric didn't follow me, but he wouldn't, would he? He was probably used to men falling at his feet the minute he touched them, and all I'd done is turn and run, or more like stumbled. It took me ten minutes of hiding behind a vast crepe myrtle, contemplating how the bush was overgrown and needed fixing, to get my head straight, and to work out what I had to do next. I needed to find Lucas and Maddie, call Spencer, get home, and then think today through, and hopefully, when I plotted it all out, I would see I'd had a small win. When I felt the coast was clear, I stepped out from the bush, but I didn't get far when a tall stranger blocked my exit. He smiled at me, but I couldn't read his expression, and I waited for him to say something. He was talking, and I snapped out of my stupid fucking internal thought process and gave him a cautious smile.

"Sorry, I didn't catch that?"

"Nick," he introduced himself and extended a hand to shake. I took his hand firmly and let it go just as quickly, but not so fast that he'd think I was an idiot.

"Brady."

"I thought it was you," Nick's smile widened. "I'm

Nick from the forum, Ash said you were coming, and it's so good to see you."

I blinked at the man. I mean, I know I did, because we all blinked, right? Nick was someone I should've known, after all, we'd chatted online a few times, but I hadn't recognized him at all.

"Oh. I didn't recognize you in real life," I offered lamely. No point in explaining that my memory had a weird kind of face blindness that I couldn't understand. I would remember Nick now that I'd seen him in person for sure, but until then I had to dig myself out of an embarrassing hole.

"We'd love to see you at the next meeting," he began.

I waited for the long explanation about how amazing it was to meet other people in my situation, and how it wasn't that far from my house, and how I should make an effort. I felt my face heat up, and I was probably scarlet. But before I could compose myself, a ripple of chatter ran through the assembled group, and it was apparent something was happening which presented as a useful excuse.

"We should go." I was relieved that I didn't have to talk any longer.

"I'd love to talk after, Brady," Nick said, and his tone was kind and dripping with compassion. Great. I was such a fucking idiot that he was feeling sorry for me. "I'll come and find you." With another smile that indicated *later*, he vanished into the group. Find me? Why would he say that? I don't want to talk to him, or find out about the support group, or get pulled to a meeting, or—

My chest was impossibly tight, and I closed my eyes, breathing through the ache of it.

"You want to find a spot for the speeches?" Eric asked from my side. Where the hell had he appeared from?

"No." I ducked his hold, and walked in the opposite direction, finding Lucas and Maddie sitting in the shade under a leafy tree with some other kids. They were having fun, chatting away about something and nothing, and even though I wanted to tell them we were leaving, I couldn't. Not when Maddie was grinning and having her hair re-styled by an older girl, nor when there were no visible signs of Lucas holding his cellphone.

So I did what I do best, I went back to my concealed corner of shrubbery to hide. In silence. Away from food, drink, chairs, Nick with his offer to chat, and more importantly, Eric with his eyes and his lips and his strong arms and his…

… everything.

Which was great until Eric found me, and smiled so hard that everything inside me turned to mush. He was so gorgeous, big, steady, and he was smiling at *me.*

I wanted to kiss that man. As Sean and Ash had kissed.

I wonder what it would be like. I practically vibrated with the heat of what I wanted, and I had no frame of reference for this. I wanted him to kiss me, to hold me tight, and make me feel a hundred times sexier than I was.

Which was why the misfiring understanding of social cues in my messed-up head spilled out, and the shit hit the fan.

FIVE

Eric

"You found my quiet spot," I teased, and then slid to a halt right in front of Brady who looked like he'd swallowed a bee or was about to pass out. "What's wrong?" I checked around us for the cause of whatever had Brady so wide-eyed. But, thank God for good reflexes, because when he launched himself at me, I had an armful of man and the only thing to do was to catch him and hold him as we stumbled back into the solid center of the big yellow bush. I didn't even get to ask what he was doing, because, without a moment's pause, he was kissing me, and fuck, could he kiss. His tongue licking into my mouth, so much heat, and I was lost in sensation, my cock hard, my hands firm on his ass, and his feet not even touching the ground. I didn't care about the rest of the guests, or the fact I was supposed to be keeping an eye on Brady, all I wanted to do was more of this kissing.

He twined his hands around my neck and gripped tight. For a few moments, he pulled back, and I thought he might've pushed me away, so I got a better hold and shifted with my thigh between his legs. He let out a soft moan and tilted his head, and the invitation was there for me to kiss him, mark him, make sure everyone knew that he was mine.

What the hell?

The kisses lasted longer each time, and I swear all it would've taken was if Brady rubbed against me for any longer, and I would be coming in my best pants. Maybe he had the same idea, or possibly he'd just run out of the immediacy of the kissing, but he broke the last one and instead rested his head on my shoulder.

"Shit," he said, with feeling.

"No, it wasn't shit." I chuckled and wondered if he wanted to stand away from me and whether I would let him go. He was way too sexy plastered to me like this, his hair smelled of lemons, and he was breathing as hard as I was.

"I've never done that before, but you touched my face," he nuzzled my neck in that super cute way that only lovers could manage. I unpicked the statement and realized he was apologizing, but I wasn't sure what for.

"I've never felt anything as hot as you jumping me, grinding down on me, and kissing me like our lives depended on it, so no apologies."

He sighed against my skin, then carefully, he extricated himself from my hold, and I had to let him go.

"It wasn't really appropriate," he murmured as he adjusted himself.

I did the same and smiled at him as I did so. "Then, I don't want to be appropriate."

"Fuck," he muttered and stepped back.

"It's okay." I could sense him withdrawing, as well as watching him back away physically, which is when he took another step away and tripped over something. What, I didn't know. I couldn't see anything there, but he sprawled this way and that, and I went to his side to offer him a hand. Only he wasn't moving; in fact, he lay there, staring at the sky, his arms extended.

I took a knee next to him. "Brady?" I asked cautiously. "Are you okay?"

He let out a noisy sigh and gripped my hand, then using me as a counterbalance to end up sitting with his legs out in front of him.

"Some people like me can't even coordinate standing up. I'm the lucky one." He clambered to his knees.

I held out my hand again, but he ignored it. I didn't understand what he was mumbling, but falling over had likely knocked the wind out of him. "You should see me after four beers," I deadpanned.

He brushed himself down and nodded. "Yeah, I need to go find the kids. Sorry about the kiss." Then, with deliberate steps, he left me standing by the bush, and I wondered what the hell had just happened.

I attempted to follow him, but Gina Lazar cornered me, and I couldn't be rude. I wanted to be, but I wasn't brought up that way.

"Hello, sexy," she said breathily and rested long scarlet talons on my arm.

"Gina," I acknowledged.

The woman was a cougar, sixty, or thereabouts. She had latched onto me and decided I was fair play to be all vampy with. She cooked a mean tuna casserole which she donated to the three of us on as many occasions as she could come up with. July Fourth, tuna casserole with a sparkler, Christmas, tuna casserole with holly, you name it, and we got it.

"Gina, you found him," Leo said from behind me, and I rounded on him in an instant. The fucker was smirking. "Eric was just telling me he hasn't had one of your casseroles in a while," Leo continued.

I narrowed my eyes at Leo, who blinked back at me as innocent as a newborn. Asshole. I felt Gina's hand track down my back and managed to shimmy away before she pinched my ass again.

"I'll make sure to bring one down to you," she smiled at me. "For absolutely no reason at all." Then she went up on tiptoes and patted my face. "Stay safe," she whispered.

As soon as she left, I turned back to Leo, but the traitor had gone. I just made a mental note to get my own back as soon as I could manage it. Then, with another soda in hand, and avoiding talking to anyone again, I ignored everyone and single-mindedly set off to find Brady with his beautiful but troubled hazel gaze, and his intriguing smile.

SIX

Brady
———————

I STABBED at the speed button on my clunky Motorola phone, and Spencer answered on the first ring.

"Hey, B," he said with all his cheerful life-is-okay enthusiasm. He was one of these bright guys whose glass was always half full, much to the annoyance of his wife Zoe who said it made arguing with him impossible. Of course when she'd said, he'd embraced her, and I'd been front row to another one of their cute married kisses. Spencer was my lifeline, the only person to see past the outward chaos that was Brady McMillan, and through to the man inside. We'd met at a grief counseling session way back after my sister died, and he'd countered my natural pessimism with so much bright energy that he broke down every one of my defenses. He was also my ride home, down here meeting with a client, and promising to be on call if I needed him. I was totally convinced he didn't even have a client near here and was only staying close just in case. I didn't know how to process how sad that made me feel, because the shame of it all burned.

"I need to leave," I blurted, and burrowed deeper into the huge bush as if it made me invisible.

"Hang on," There was some rustling, and then Spencer was back. "What happened?'

"Nothing. Everything. I'm so fucked."

"Count down from one hundred—"

"I don't need that, I'm calm, sort of. I fell over."

There was a long pause. "Okay, well that doesn't sound too bad, was it in front of people? It's a wedding; people fall over all the time when the champagne starts to flow. No one will have noticed."

"It was in front of one important person," I snapped, "and I didn't get up, I was mortified, and I just lay there staring up at the sky like an idiot."

"Important person? One of the grooms?"

I could have kicked myself that I'd even used that stupid word. "No, one of Ash's friends, Eric."

"Okay, is Eric the cop?"

"No, the firefighter, that's not important. He was talking to me and shit," I rubbed at my eyes, and slumped back even more. "I kissed him."

"Fuck, yes!" Spencer announced with enthusiasm, "wait, he kissed you, or you kissed him?"

"Shit, Spencer."

"Okay, it's okay. I'm ten minutes away, do you need me to come and get you and the kids?" Unspoken was the question—*how bad are you right now?*

I hated that Spencer had to deal with my shit. DCD was the bane of my fucking life. It's one of those things that made me look like I'd been drinking even when I hadn't, and I'd just fucked up with Eric in several ways. I was aware that in the grand scheme of things I was one of the lucky ones, my DCD could've been way worse, and this single truth was what my mom had drummed into me as I was growing up. I'd gotten a diagnosis, but when the specialists had told my distraught mother that others had worse cases, then that was the positive she'd taken hold of. Maybe that was why I was friends with Spencer and his sunshine outlook on life.

My mom had been convinced DCD was a gift from God that meant I could draw the world around me. Even if I believed in an almighty being, which I didn't, I hadn't been given a gift. No, what I had was a curse that weakened me. Take today, for instance. My low self-esteem was a hammer that crashed into my skull at various moments, and walking back from Eric and ending up on my ass was a slam to the brain that left me feeling like a fucking idiot. I could've sat on the ground and wept at the sheer crappiness of it all.

Then when he'd rushed over to help me, I'd just wanted to curl into a ball and tell him to go away. I didn't want his help; I'd wanted to be able to sashay my gay ass away from a man I was interested in without crumbling to the damn ground.

Someone like Eric wouldn't be interested in someone like *me*, and not only was I falling over, I'd assaulted the poor guy. There was no *probably* about it. I owed him an apology, and I would find him just as we were leaving to tell him, preferably from a distance, with a table between us, and Maddie and Lucas at my side. Men like Eric, big strong hero-types, were my kryptonite, and they only ever got with me because they wanted to fix me, there was no way he could give me what I needed. A hero who loved me with all my flaws, and not just the parts of me that worked to their version of okay.

So, yeah, I'm done here.

"Brady, are you there? Do you want me to come?"

"Yeah?"

"Are you sure? You said this Ash guy is kind, and you're friends. Why don't you—"

"The kids want to leave."

He didn't sigh, but there was a noticeable pause, which made me feel as if he was judging me. He wasn't, he wouldn't do that, but I'm an expert at filling spaces with the most horrific thoughts. "I'll text you when I'm outside. Don't worry about things."

I ended the call, shoving the phone into my pocket, and pushing at it hard when it didn't slip in. It was so old that I should've been more careful, but I just needed to get myself out of here.

"You're leaving already?" Ash said from right next to me.

Shit, how much had he heard? I faced my online friend and wished I could read his expression correctly.

"The kids have… stuff."

"You look like you're ready to run," Ash murmured, and waved a hand in front of him, probably to indicate me running, or something.

I wished I was online, and this was a conversation in the ether.

With a screen between us, I might even have been able to talk out my fears, and if the speech recognition software made out what I was trying to say, I might have been able to explain what had happened. I would've explained what I'd done to poor Eric, and how he was a nice guy, and how I was a complete fucking idiot. I might even have talked about being in a social situation that was messing with my head and asked for Ash's advice. Not that I'd ever done that with Ash, I was adept at making sure conversations were focused back on him, and with a wedding to plan, it had been easy. But Ash was a foot away from me, and I was lost.

"It's probably time for me to go as well," I said after a pause. I waited for him to tell me I was silly, that I should stay, and have fun, whatever that meant. Instead, he pulled me into a hug which was unnerving and yet oddly comforting.

"Will you meet up with me? When we get back from the honeymoon?"

I closed my eyes then, because if I couldn't see his face, then it was as if he couldn't see me. Stupid, I know, but I was done with the day.

"That would be great," I lied again, with added forced enthusiasm.

"Did Eric look after you okay?"

"Huh?"

"I asked him to keep an eye out, make sure you were okay."

The shock of this admission was hard to take. For a few moments, I thought I'd actually had a normal conversation with a hot guy, and that he'd actually wanted to get me food and drink. The bitterness spilled into my words.

"He took great care of me. Thank you for organizing that."

"It's time, Ash," purple-hat-lady said, from among a group of chattering people past the end of the path, all armed with champagne flutes.

"You should go," I encouraged. "Eat cake, give the best speech."

He squeezed my hand and followed the woman, and then, with shoulders back, I headed for where I'd seen Lucas and Maddie sitting.

Only, getting close to them was impossible when Eric was in my way. I didn't think he was trying to be in my way, but he couldn't help it, he was at the very least half a foot taller than me, broad, solidly built, and the path through the bushes wasn't all that wide.

"Hey," he said, and his face split in a wide smile. "I was looking for you."

"Why?" I asked, feeling hemmed in, even though I could've turned around and walked the other way.

"I wanted to say, if I messed up, or said something, then I'm sorry. Sean is always saying that—"

"What?" I stared at him with shock.

"Huh?" Cue him being confused. "What do you mean, what?"

Were we talking in circles? I didn't want to talk to him.

"Why are you apologizing to *me*?" I asked. "You didn't do anything. It was me that… y'know…"

He shrugged and smiled at me, "Can I take you to dinner?"

Great, last thing I needed was a pity thing because newly married Ash thought I was lonely or something.

"Tell Ash his concern is noted and thanks, but no thanks. Now I need to get the kids, can you move?"

I stepped to one side and brushed past him, and was gone before he had time to process. The kids didn't want to leave, but I promised them Spencer would stop to take us all to McDonald's on the way home, and we left when everyone was distracted by speeches, laughter, love, and cake.

And yeah, yet again I was missing out.

SEVEN

Eric

BRADY NEVER LEFT my thoughts even when I was back at work. It had been three days since the wedding, and I couldn't get the kiss out of my head, or the action we'd had up against the tree. Brady hadn't stood there and let me drive that kiss—it had been fire and passion and need, and fuck, I was getting hard every time I thought about it. Clearly, he didn't want to know me, but I couldn't shake what had happened from my mind.

"Earth to Eric? Adam texted to say he's coming in today," Frankie interrupted my thoughts, and I realized I was sitting on the bench, staring into space.

"Huh?" I stood and closed my locker, which I'd been staring into for quite some time, thinking through what I was going to say when I called Brady. Because I was determined to make him see that dinner, or something, was an excellent idea. The impetus to connect with him was a small spark inside me that I couldn't extinguish.

"Adam says he's bringing a couple of kids in with him, for our usual meeting."

Our shift didn't start for another thirty minutes, and Adam would've known that, choosing this particular time to visit and catch us all in place. Not one of us tried to avoid what he had planned because it had been a collective idea. After being injured in an RTA rescue this time last year, Adam was still riding a desk, with only a little hope of active duty again. After weeks of dark times, it had been Sean's idea that Adam begin a program for connecting kids who'd been victims of fire, or accidents, or who just needed adult support from someone who had known trauma. Adam had balked at the idea at first, then he'd met a few of the children, and now that was his thing. He covered admin at the firehouse, but he also worked on his big brother support program.

Hence today's visit. We all knew about the newest additions to the program, twins aged twelve who had lost everything in a house fire.

"Guys?" Adam called from the locker room door, and we headed out with enthusiasm. "This is Annabelle and Mikey; they wanted to meet you." The tell-tale burn scars on Mikey's arms were all we needed to see to remind us of what he'd seen, but none of us commented. We launched right into messing with Adam, and making Annabelle and Mikey smile.

"How are you doing?" I asked Adam when he was getting coffee, away from the kids. There was a flash of frustration in his eyes, but he wouldn't let loose in front of Annabelle and Mikey.

"I want to come back," he shrugged.

"You will," I encouraged, believing that miracles can happen. He was lucky to be alive, and a goddamn hero for what he'd done, getting a child out of a car just seconds before a bridge support crushed it. He could have followed the rules and waited for us, but the victim would have died, and anyway, he'd reacted as any of us would've. He'd seen the danger and put the life of a trapped boy before his. He deserved more for what he'd done, more than a commendation, but getting back on active duty wasn't going to happen anytime soon.

"I'm volunteering at Ringwood this weekend," he said.

"I'll be there if I can."

Ringwood was a foster home out on Murphy Canyon Road, and the three of us, plus Adam now, volunteered our time when we could, gardening, building, anything where they needed help.

"Guys, we're being called out," Dale, lead firefighter of our team, announced. Our time was up, and Adam, Annabelle, and Mikey watched as we peeled out of the station.

"Adam seems good," Parker commented.

Gemma was quiet, she always was after seeing Adam, after all, she'd been the one to take his place, and I could understand her feelings. No one wanted to fill another firefighter's shoes.

"He is good," I half-lied. He had most of his world sorted out, but I thought I could tell that the need to be on active duty was eating away at him. Unless I was projecting, because the idea of not being a firefighter filled me with dread.

Within thirty minutes, we were at the Command site staring out at the wall of the newest fire, named *Bullhead*, for the creek where it had originated. It jumped and spat in the far distance, tearing through stands of bug-killed trees. This wasn't as big as the fucker we'd been fighting all last week, but it wasn't looking good.

The commander called for our attention. "Okay, brush two-seven, it has a good wind on it, and a critical rate of spread. The town has four hundred souls. You're relieving twelve evac which is being moved to assist with the fire up the ridge." He heaved a sigh.

"The fucking witching hour," Frankie summarized, yanking on his jacket with focused aggression.

He was the most superstitious member of the five-person group that formed this particular CALFIRE bush team. Dale was the firefighter in charge, broody, serious, and the man you wanted at your back. Gemma was the newest, transferred in from a posting in Colorado but well experienced in some of the worst that Mother Nature threw at firefighters. She was nodding along with the whole witching hour summary, and to be honest, Frankie was only saying what we were all thinking.

"By the time we hike into town there, we'll be past it," I attempted to diffuse the situation because that was my role, quiet and level-headed, the steady man on the team. No one on the engine crew wanted to think about the perfect storm we could be walking into. The late afternoon was the most dangerous time for the people fighting a wildfire when the sun is hot, relative humidity is low, and when, like now, the winds are high, hence the name the witching hour.

Parker, the final member of our team, shrugged.

"Witching hour or whatever, it's a fire, and we can deal with it."

He was Mr. Positive, the one who stuck to his belief he could handle anything. I liked him for his sunny, bright outlook on life, and he was the joker of the five of us. Not that he'd managed to prank me yet, given I lived with Leo who'd tried most things to irritate me. I was used to Leo's shit, so there was no way Parker could win one over me.

Dale climbed back into the cab. "Weather front's moving in," he confirmed. It hadn't taken long for the guys in charge of resources to give Dale the information, because he hadn't been gone for more than five minutes. He had a map which he held up, and began to confirm the information we needed—fire status, weather conditions, watch-out situations, and lastly, escape routes.

"We could get a shift in wind direction, and they're telling dispatch that radio communication is spotty, so I want eyes open, and we're sweeping from the first ranch, down to the houses, and taking the service road to get back in a circle. We have an hour to get this done and get out. Are we good?"

"Yes, sir," we chorused.

We *were* good. This was our job, and to a non-firefighter, this was a fact that was often difficult to understand. I wasn't scared of getting into the small town. I was respectful of the fire and knew that with deference and a healthy dose of luck, we would be fine, and *that* was the difference. Fire was unpredictable, needy, cruel, and worst of all I'd seen it kill on more than one occasion, but we were trained professionals.

We were spread thin, though. Just because there were fires in the hills, didn't mean there weren't things to attend to in the city, but when a wall of flame was heading toward towns, we were an essential cog in the wheel. We'd seen it all, even the aftermath of the Paradise fire, which was indelibly etched into my memory. We'd lost so many people that day, civilians, firefighters, and the lessons learned had shifted the whole process of firefighting, although whether it had been enough, we wouldn't know until the next disaster hit.

Fire wasn't something anyone could one hundred percent plan for anyway. It didn't burn straight, and it didn't follow a path that we could stop in its tracks. It jumped and ran and flew from acre to acre in a sometimes erratic pattern. A firefighter had to make educated guesses, and on occasion, the fire won.

The Bullhead fire was new, unpredictable, and even though models said the town of Lewens had to be evacuated, the fire might not even head this way. Flames crowned and jumped from one treetop to the next and burning embers started spot fires. Before long, the central fire caught up with the spots and then everything blended in a fast-moving wall of heat — a fire tsunami.

We drove past people leaving town, the ones who were smart, or scared enough to know to evacuate, cars with kids and animals inside, some of the drivers acknowledging us as we drove in. Frankie and I took the first call, ensuring the ranch on the outskirts was empty, it seemed derelict as it was, and it stood in a clear area, so we moved on rapidly, until one by one we'd gotten to maybe three houses from the end. The air was smoky, and the wind direction had changed. We knew that, but we had to trust that Command had control of the information. We'd had no call to leave, and Dale wasn't unduly worried.

The last house going out of town was a one-story set back from the road, the yard immaculate, the little place pretty and well-maintained, and on the stoop, arms folded over her chest, was a woman who wasn't leaving.

There were procedures for this, a *mandatory* evacuation was just that, but in California, there was such a thing as evacuation fatigue. Lewens had been evacuated twice this year already, and both times the fire had turned, and some townspeople had reached the point where they were happy to take their chances.

"They're calling us out," Dale informed as Frankie and I left the engine. "Get her, and whatever is holding her here, and let's get the hell out of Dodge."

Frankie followed me over to the small woman with a stubborn tilted chin, whose body language screamed for us to go.

"Louella Herrera. Get off my property," she said before I could even open my mouth.

"Mandatory evacuation," Frankie responded evenly. He was always more diplomatic than me in situations like this. I would be tempted to pick her up, throw her over my shoulder, and force her into the truck, but he was all about the calm approach.

"Third time this season," Louella snapped.

"What's keeping you here, ma'am?" Frankie inquired, in his best we-totally-understand voice.

"I don't drive, and there are two cats in carriers, one arthritic dog, sixty years of memories, and my husband's ashes spread in the land out back."

Frankie nodded. "Fetch the dog, Eric and I will get the cats, get them into the truck, you have the memories in your head, and your husband wouldn't want you dying next to him."

She eyed him suspiciously, and I held my breath. I was all ready to pick her up at that point when her shoulders slumped.

"This time's for real?" she asked.

"Wind's turned," Frankie explained as if we had all the time in the world, which we fucking didn't.

She turned from us, indicated two cat carriers, and put her ancient and placid dog on a leash, hoisted a backpack on her shoulder, then shut and locked her door.

"Let's go," she said and marched toward the engine as if it'd been her idea to leave.

Frankie and I exchanged glances, took a cat carrier each, then followed her, and within a minute or two of stopping we were back and heading for the service road. Louella sat next to Frankie, across from me, staring out of the window, sadness marking her face. We could see the fire, dancing at the top of the valley, maybe three miles away.

"It's closer than any other time," Louella whispered, tears welling in her eyes. Her dog, a lab-collie mix, rested his head on her lap, and she scuffed behind his ears. "I'm done," she said and leaned over her dog, kissing his head.

We made it back to the main road and back to Command with time to spare, everyone pulled back to this position. The Hotshots had burned a break line, but the town of Lewens had to be sacrificed when the fire raced so fast it couldn't be saved.

We watched the town burn on the monitors, news bulletins that spoke of no fatalities, that evacuation had been smooth.

Louella was picked up by her frantic daughter an hour after we'd gotten her out, demanding her mom relocate to Seattle with her, where it rained a lot, and she'd be safer.

Last I heard from Louella, apart from a soft thank you to Frankie and me, was a disgruntled explanation to her daughter about Seattle—earthquakes, volcanoes, and tsunamis. Night had fallen, bringing an otherworldly calm as it began to rain gently. It wouldn't be enough to stop the fire, but the flaming beast had reached the point where Command confirmed they had it somewhat contained. We were done, and when I arrived home a little after three in the morning, Leo was ready with coffee and broad shoulders in case I needed to talk, and a bottle of whiskey if it had been so bad that I needed to drink my grief away.

"Just coffee," I said, and he handed it to me.

I took the drink out into the garden past the pool to the chairs, and Leo came with me. Cap wound in and out of my legs and I was so tired I nearly stepped on him twice. Leo sat next to me in his usual chair; the third one, Sean's place, was empty, but he'd be back from his honeymoon soon. We still kept it there, because even though he lived next door, he still joined us some evenings when he wasn't ready to take the horrors of his day back to Ash without working through them first. We spent some time in silence, and then Cap dropped a Frisbee in my lap with an insistent woof.

"Your dog is stupid," I summarized, "He knows it's dark, right?"

Leo snorted a laugh. "You're his favorite Frisbee guy, what can I say?"

I stroked his head and then leaned down to speak to him. "Cap, you're an idiot. It's three a.m.. It's not Frisbee time."

He let out a soft whine, so I took the toy and threw it randomly into the darkness. I heard it hit the pool, and the subsequent splash as dog hit water. Next to me, Leo groaned.

"You did *not* throw that in the pool, asshole."

"You clearly missed me explaining that it's dark," I said with a smile.

"I'm letting him into your room."

"You wouldn't dare."

"Believe me, I would," Leo said, and we both yelped when Cap dropped the Frisbee onto my lap and then shook. Water went everywhere, Cap woofed in delight, and for just a few moments I could relax.

"Leo, can I ask a favor?"

Leo turned his head to look at me. "No."

"I didn't even ask yet."

"The last time you asked me a favor I couldn't get away from Gina, and she force-fed me tuna casserole."

I snorted a laugh because that had been some funny shit, Leo coming back stinking of tuna, and explaining how Gina had suggested that she needed to be strip-searched by a cop because it was on her bucket list. I've never seen Leo so wide-eyed in my entire life.

"This is different. You know Ash's friend, Brady?"

"What about him?"

"He's in my head," I finally offered.

I recalled the moment he'd leaped at me and kissed me, and the way he'd tumbled to the ground, and the resignation in him, and the fear. I couldn't stop thinking about him, and I needed to see him, although why I couldn't explain.

Leo leaned toward me. "For real?"

All I could do was shrug. "Seems that way, although I don't have no idea if it's for real, or just an itch or what, but there was something about him, a fear, a need, shit…" I scrubbed at my eyes and was pleased I was only talking to Leo because I sounded like a damn idiot.

"You don't do needy guys, remember? We talked about this hero-complex you have going on."

"Ha fucking ha, I'm serious here."

"What are you going to do about it?" he asked after a pause in which I could imagine his brain working.

"Get myself up to his place and visit."

Leo let out a noisy sigh and settled back in his chair. "Fuck my life. First Sean and now you?"

"I don't get your problem. You can always date Gina."

He punched me hard in the arm, the asshole, and I punched him back. That started Cap jumping around us like a mad thing—damp stinky dog was not the best thing to have flicked in your face. When Cap stopped dancing, and Leo and I stopped wrestling like idiots, we both sat back with our coffee.

"I'm going the day after tomorrow unless I get a call in, but I need his address, that's the favor in case you didn't know. I mean I'd get it myself, but it doesn't seem right."

And all I got from Leo?

"Not a fucking chance."

EIGHT

Brady

WHEN I ANSWERED THE DOOR, Spencer thrust a box at me. "I need help," he announced, and sidled past me, heading straight for the kitchen and helping himself to coffee.

"Help with what?" I examined the box, seeing sheets of paper. A lot of paper.

"Stapling," he said, then opened the cupboard for the cereals and searching for the Captain Crunch I kept just for him. He sometimes did this, turning up before breakfast with some mission or other, so that I'd see him.

Carefully, I considered how I was going to close the door and then take the heavy box to the table.

Move sideways a little. Use your hip to bump the door. Balance yourself. Hold the box. Stop and breathe. Move toward the table slowly. Remember, it's seven steps from door to table. Relax. Breathe some more.

When the box was settled, I felt a hundred kinds of accomplished and turned to face my friend, who was stuffing his face with sugary squares.

"It's for The Light Club," he said, "I need them for the next meeting."

The Light Club was where we'd met, the grief counseling had lasted a year, and I left, but Spencer had stayed, working through the grief of losing his parents close together from cancer, and in time becoming the leader of the group. An accountant by trade, he always said he loved seeing the hearts of people rather than the dryness of numbers. Yep, he was always poetic, as well as bright, and sometimes far too loud this early in the day.

I lifted out the top sheaf of papers, and flicked through what I could see was a notebook of sorts.

"It's a journal," Spencer explained, and put down the cereal long enough to help me get the rest of the paper out. "Each page is a different color, and I need it stapled in rainbow order. You want to help?" He pulled out two staplers, "I bought you your own stapler. I'll even get you coffee."

I made a show of sighing, but he knew I was only joking, and he grinned at me before bringing back a fresh cup of caffeine. I had exactly two cups of coffee a day, any more than that and it made me all kinds of weird, hyper even. One specialist said way back, that I probably had a weak attention span, ADHD, that I was on the autistic spectrum, oh and it wasn't likely I'd ever live an independent life.

My mom sued him. Or at least had threatened to. I'd been very young, and all I recall is her hugging me and telling me I was everything I was meant to be. When the DCD diagnosis had happened, and she'd given me that whole thing about how it could have been worse, I guess it could have been. I'd lived on my own for an entire year, started my own company, found my happy place, before coming back here for Maddie and Lucas. Now *they* were my happy place and everything I wanted.

"So, pink first, then peach, then lemon, then lime, then pale blue. Okay?"

I collected the five pieces of paper and carefully lined them up before stapling the corner. In the time it had taken me to do one, I swear Spencer had ten, but fuck that, he never judged me, and I felt like a paper-sorting-ninja. We chatted about inconsequential things, like the weather, and the fact that his son, Liam, the same age as Lucas, was also wearing a lot of deodorant. That part we exchanged in whispers because there was no way we wanted Lucas to hear us giggling like kids.

"So, about this guy you kissed?"

I stapled my current stack of paper and then shook my head. "I was insane." I could feel the heat in my face.

"Did I ever tell you about what I did with Zoe?"

"A hundred times," I reminded him. "You were drunk at an end-of-term beach barbecue. You kissed her and then she shoved you in a lake."

"So it worked out for me."

A sigh escaped me. "It's a good bet I'll never see him again."

Spencer made a big show of straightening papers, then cleared his throat. "I think it would be good if you made an effort to see him again, or at least contact him, or maybe visit your friend Ash."

"Good for whom?" I laughed and passed him the final papers I'd stapled.

"Good for *you*, Brady."

"I will," I lied.

"Okay, then."

When Spencer left, he hugged me before picking up the box and escaped just as the kids were stirring upstairs. He meant well, coming over with projects that worked on my dexterity and coordination skills, being a friend, even asking me to get over myself and visit Ash, and of course, Eric. When his car reversed off the drive, I felt bereft. That had been the perfect opportunity for me to talk about the confusion of feelings I had for Eric, and I know Spencer would never bullshit me.

Even when I was organizing the kids' lunch bags, I couldn't shake the feeling I'd missed out on a good chance for Spencer to tell me I hadn't messed up, and for me to actually believe him.

Peace didn't last long at all. Lucas was first downstairs, and he was pissed. Not with me, or with life in general, but with his little sister.

"Maddie deleted my playlist, and I'm going to kill her," Lucas informed me. Standing in what had been his mom's kitchen, with his arms crossed over his chest, he was a mini-Nicole, and a flash of grief stole my breath.

I missed Nicole so much, more than I ever imagined I might. When she'd moved out, gone to college, met Dan, had the kids, I thought we wouldn't see each other much. She'd been my best friend, hell she'd often been my only friend for most of my childhood, but college was her rite of passage, and she needed to do it. College wasn't on my list, but I understood the distance between us.

Until she'd died and the distance became insurmountable.

"I'm sure she didn't mean to," I soothed.

"Spencer got Liam his own Spotify account," Lucas added, "then there's no way his stupid sister can delete his stuff."

"How did she even get on the family Spotify when you're the only one who uses it, and it's on the phone which is permanently welded to your side?"

He shook his head and rolled his eyes, a pretty standard look for him these days, whenever I do or say something that is in his eyes, old-guy talk.

"It's on the computer too," he added the *duh* expression again.

"I didn't see her on the computer."

"You were in the shower, and anyway, she doesn't have a phone or a computer, and she needed *someone* to help her with her math, and you couldn't do it, so I let her on my computer to look up how to do something, and she deleted everything."

There was a lot of information in that announcement. There was the subtle dig that yes, I couldn't help the kids too much with homework, and also that Maddie didn't have her own computer. How did I explain to Lucas that I was scared to let her have her own because I wouldn't be able to police it? What would he say if I told him that it had taken me an entire night of losing my shit with Ash over chat about Lucas getting a computer before he'd calmed me down. Finally, I'd given in—the kids needed a way to access the world, anything to give them what I couldn't. One computer in the front room for Lucas, right where I could see it was my compromise.

Paisley, in her very particular therapist kind of way, told me I had all the tools to unlock both confidence and my abilities to communicate. In her words, I wasn't trying hard enough and that I was clearly doing something wrong somewhere. What that thing was we hadn't discovered yet, but I resented her every month when I visited, only to be told about my untapped potential.

"Okay, I'll talk to… someone… about… something."

Fuck my life, could I sound any lamer?

Lucas sighed, and then nodded., "There's nothing anyone can do, I'll just have to remake the playlists," he left me standing in the kitchen to think about how I hadn't dealt with his crisis at all.

It used to be so easy. Feed them. Play with them. Buy their clothes. Make them happy with little games. Tell them made-up stories at bedtime. Then Lucas had turned twelve, and somehow he thought that the entire universe conspired to ride his ass.

"I didn't mean to," Maddie said from the doorway, her eyes bright with emotion, her teddy grasped in her hands. She was on the cusp of something as well, still a small child in so many ways, then switching on a dime to wanting and needing to grow up. Right at that moment, she was still that small person who I could connect with.

"I know you didn't, sweetheart," I said, and she ran to me. Leaning against the counter, I could easily catch her and swing her up to hug her briefly before planting her butt next to the microwave.

"I wanted to listen to Justin Timberlake," she began, "and I pressed these buttons and it asked me if I was sure, and I was sure I wanted to listen to Justin, and then it was all gone." She sighed, and I hugged her close, Juniper Teddy between us, before setting her back and looking at the toy. He had fur missing in a few places, one of his eyes lost, but he was still the last thing Nicole and Dan had bought for her, and I'd spun so many stories at bedtime about Juniper and his adventures that he had a life all of his own.

"Lucas knows you didn't mean it."

"He doesn't, he shouted at me."

Her lower lip trembled, and I attempted to stop her from getting any sadder. Changing the subject would help. "You want pancakes for breakfast?" I asked.

She brightened visibly. "Chocolate?"

"Blueberry?"

"Chocolate *and* blueberry?"

I laughed at her negotiation techniques, and the mood was broken. With Juniper propped up on the side watching us with his one beady eye, we made pancakes, and I called out for Lucas when they were done.

He sauntered in as if chocolate and blueberry pancakes weren't his absolute favorite thing, and the smell of Lynx body spray followed him in a wafting cloud. Twelve seemed to be the age of deodorant and body spray, often in quantities that would make an average person's eyes water. I wondered if maybe there was a girl at school, because he was taking a lot of showers, and had lamented that his sneakers weren't Nike but a generic brand. I could get him what he wanted, money wasn't the issue, but he'd never been interested in brands before.

"Did you want to say something to your sister?" I pressed.

"Sorry I shouted," Lucas' response was immediate and heartfelt. They were close as siblings, and Lucas took after his mom, who'd been quick to temper and just as fast to harmony.

"Sorry I pressed buttons," Maddie replied.

They exchanged smiles, and the knot that had been tightening in my chest unraveled. Everything was back to normal, they were eating breakfast, and I could relax. I added finding someone who knew computers to the list of things I couldn't do for the kids I'd been entrusted with. Maybe Ash would know someone, given he worked with computers better than I did, and that went on the list of things to talk to Ash about when he came back from his honeymoon.

Not that I'd entirely forgotten the fact he'd sicced his friend on me with the order to look after me — the ass.

My mind wandered back to Eric and the kiss, and I flushed scarlet as I did every damn time. I've never had a kiss like it, not one where I took control or demanded something real from another man. God knows what I'd been thinking.

"Can I get twenty dollars for lunch?" Lucas asked.

"Haven't you already had—?"

"I spent it because I needed new folders—"

"Why twenty?" I asked, because really?

"Never mind, Uncle Brady," he said, with his best stoic expression and a smile, "I'll ask Grandpa to transfer me some."

"Don't be silly," I pulled a twenty from my wallet. At

least I had a twenty in there, I could have sworn I had more, but who knew if I remembered right. I seemed to be spending it like water, mostly on things for Maddie and Lucas. This just made my newest commission even more critical, and I needed to get my head out of thinking about Eric and back on essential things.

First, I needed to stop recalling Eric's eyes as I got myself off in the shower. Or his hold when I pulled lube from my bedside table and fingered myself before coming over my belly.

Lucas hugged me from the side. "Thank you," he murmured, and my heart melted. He may have been a snotty almost-teenager, but he did love me in his own way. The rest of the before-school routine went smoothly, and when they left to get on the bus, I almost felt like I'd managed to do everything right.

I was taking the win.

NINE

Eric

"What's up?" Leo asked from behind me and scared me so much I yelped. I'd been so engrossed in trying out different passwords that I'd forgotten Leo was due home at ten tonight.

"Nothing," I slammed the lid shut, just in time when Cap leaped off the couch where he'd been curled next to me, and threw himself at Leo and demanded attention. The two of them did this crazy dog and doggy dad dance, then Leo vanished into the kitchen, coming back with two beers and going straight into the garden. I followed, with Cap trailing us both, a Frisbee in his mouth and his tail wagging so hard he could barely walk in a straight line.

We took our usual chairs, staring out into the dark, and Leo didn't talk at first. I was happy to sit there and chill with him, get him to shake free from whatever headspace he was in at the moment. It was up to Leo to talk first, and it took a while.

"Arrested a guy today," he said.
"Uh-huh."

Leo sighed heavily, swallowed a mouthful of beer, and then petted Cap some more. I thought maybe that was all I was getting, and that was fine, the three of us, me, Leo, and Sean, had this way of supporting and understanding without saying a word.

"Human trafficking," he said after the longest time.

I could only imagine what it was he'd seen. Last spring, I'd attended a structure fire next to a trailer and the horrors I'd seen had sent me in a tailspin that lasted a long time. The pictures in my mind would never leave, but that was okay, it's what we'd all signed up for, and we each had our way of dealing with things. For me, when things got too bad, I drank away the horror, which wasn't half as physically and spiritually healthy as Leo, who prayed and went for long walks with Cap, to escape his demons.

He didn't elaborate on his day, but he raised his bottle to mine, and we clinked them. What we were toasting I didn't know. It could've been a job well done, or a success, a failure, or even remembering those we couldn't save. It was just enough that we were doing it.

"Saw your dad up on the podium again," he added to the silence.

"What now?" I loved my dad, but being the son of Senator Lester-Hythe left me wide open to Leo teasing me.

"Social reform, blah blah, boys in blue, but he did shake my hand and asked after his only child, and lamented that said only child hadn't been home to see Mom in a while."

"I was there last week, and he knows it, and Mom knows it, and ignore him."

"I did. Your dad, he's one of the good guys," Leo murmured, "and you know I love your mom."

"So do I, and I'll visit on my next day off."

After the beer was done, we went back into the house, and Leo picked up the laptop I'd closed.

"Spill," he shook the laptop in front of me.

"What?" I forced an expression of innocence and hoped it would work, but Leo knew me so well.

"Ash left his laptop here for us to look after, not to hack into."

"I wasn't hacking," I lied, but I'd never had a very good poker face.

"What passwords did you try?"

"I wasn't—"

"You know I'm a cop, right? I know his password, and if you tell me what you want to see, then I might let you know."

I drew myself taller. I was a head taller than Leo and twice as wide, and he knew that if it came to it, I'd be the one sitting on him and tickling him until he cried and *begged* to give me the password. He raised a single eyebrow and silently dared me to even try it. I chose the path of least resistance.

"I wanted to look at that forum," I explained. "I tried on my laptop, but you have to be a member to talk to other members."

"For a reason, you ass, it's private, and what you really mean is that you want to talk to Brady specifically," he said.

I shook my head. "So what if I do."

"Jesus, what are you? Nine?" He sat down and patted

for me to sit next to him, which wasn't easy as Cap got there first, then he opened the laptop and typed in the password he had in his head. "You want to check out his porn?" he asked.

I wrenched the laptop from him. "What are you? Sixteen?"

He sniggered and then settled in for the duration. I knew damn well he'd be watching me. I knew I was wrong to do this. What if Brady thought I was Ash, what if he told Ash what I was doing, what if... I closed the laptop and slid it back in its case.

"If it helps, I didn't get his address."

"You didn't?"

"I texted you this afternoon, did you not see it?"

"My phone is dead."

Leo rolled his eyes. "Your phone is always freaking dead. I wonder why I bother." Then he elbowed me. "I would have broken a hundred laws getting his address, and you know it could be construed as stalking."

"It's not stalking when he kissed me first, right?"

Leo laughed and slid down the seat, closing his eyes. "Who are you trying to convince?"

"I don't want his address," I decided there and then. "That would be wrong, but how else am I going to convince him to see me again?"

"Easy, get Sean to ask Ash to ask Brady if it's okay for you to call to arrange a you visit, simple."

That didn't sound very simple to me, but I pulled up my iPad and hit Facetime to connect to Sean and Ash. I mean, it was ten p.m., they were on their honeymoon, what could they be doing that was more important than getting me some time with Brady?

Mia answered the call. Or at least Ash or Sean did, only it was Mia's face in the frame, I repositioned the iPad so she could see both me and Leo.

"Nen, Fido, Fido" she babbled and slapped the screen. A distinctly adult hand helped her away, and then Sean's face filled the screen.

"Wassup?" he asked, and concern filled his voice.

"You busy?" I asked, and next to me, Leo snorted.

"It's my honeymoon," Sean began patiently, "yes, I'm busy."

"I can clearly see that Mia is awake," I pointed out.

Sean leaned into the iPad, and then there was movement as if he was taking it out of the room. "She *wasn't.*"

"My bad," I muttered, and Leo couldn't stop laughing, sniggering away next to me.

"What do you need that is so important you woke up Mia and interrupted my champagne and strawberries time with Ash."

"TMI dude," I muttered.

"We'd only just got her to sleep and closed the door, and I forgot to turn down the ring on the damn iPad. Lesson learned, Eric, lesson learned."

"Will you hmm..." I side-eyed Leo who was shaking so hard with silent laughter that I reckoned with one good shove he'd be on the floor. Which I did, sending him sprawling on the rug, Cap climbing all over him.

"Spit it out, E," Sean said, and I saw him glance behind

him, "yeah, it's Eric," I heard him say to Ash. "No, nothing important babe, put the champagne back in the ice."

"Can you ask Brady if it's okay for me to visit and can I have his address."

"Brady?"

"Long story."

"What do you want… wait… I don't have his address. I know he lives about forty minutes north of here."

"Will you get Ash to go online now for me?"

"Now? What the fuck, dude?"

"Please."

Sean stared right into the camera, narrowed his eyes, and didn't say a thing. He just stared at me as if he was sizing up the situation and had a hundred different scenarios running through his head. Then he sighed with great exaggeration. "Okay, asshole, I'll do it now, but you owe me a month of babysitting."

"Happy to do it," I said immediately. Babysitting Mia was a treat, not a punishment.

He ended the call, and I sat back on the couch. That was all I could do, wait for Sean to do his thing. Knowing my luck, Brady would take one look at the request and throw his own laptop out of the window.

"Now what?" Leo asked from the rug.

"Now nothing, we wait, I guess." Waiting is super hard; waiting is not something I'm overly good at.

"Hey, did you hear Mia's new word?"

"No," I lied because this joke was a long game, and I had a play all worked out.

"Fido?" he said and frowned. "I wonder what that means? It must be something super clever."

I didn't know how I kept a straight face—little did Leo know that he would forever be called Uncle Five-Oh. Or maybe we'd just leave it as Fido.

A message popped up on the screen from Sean, a screencap of an exchange between Ash and Brady. Just seeing Brady's name sent a thrill of excitement through me, and I knew I had it bad. The message had an address, and a phone number, with an extra note that I could call him to arrange a visit.

Which is exactly what I neglected to do.

TEN

Brady

THE EXCHANGE with Ash last night had me restless in sleep. It wasn't so much that I couldn't sleep only that my dreams morphed from bizarre to erotic. Why did Eric want to know where I lived? I'd waited for a text from Eric, one that I could answer with a simple thanks but no thanks, but nothing had arrived yet, so I guessed I'd have to deal with that when it happened and put everything out of my head. Sitting in my office and contemplating the day ahead, I even managed to forget, which was a feat in itself. I had nothing to be worried about, nothing to be ashamed of, and I could happily go through life and never see Eric again.

My office was nothing more than a small area with a door off the main bedroom, the part of the room where Nicole had an above garage addition creating a walk-in closet area. It had a tiny window which opened, with views over the park if you were standing, and a skylight in the roof, so the space was flooded with sunshine. I'd had the bars and shelves removed, or rather, I'd removed them myself in a paroxysm of grief. A month after Nicole and

Dan had died, when the children had decided they wanted to go back to school, I'd taken a mallet, and I'd destroyed it all, had thrown everything out of the window into the backyard. Then I'd sat curled in the corner crying for as long as it took me to realize the kind of precious things I might have thrown out in my distress.

Nicole's purses, filled with receipts, notes, lipsticks; Dan's ties, his dress uniform, a scrapbook of photos. It had taken me the rest of the day, but I'd packed everything I'd thrown out neatly into boxes, and put them in the attic for the children to have when they were older. How I'd managed it I didn't know, but somehow I'd had focus, and as soon as I could find a contractor who could fix the mess I'd made of the walls, I'd decided to make the space my own. For the longest time, the rest of the house had stayed the same, artwork, ornaments, photos; everything was as Nicole and Dan had left it. It wasn't easy keeping it like that though.

For that spread of years, lack of change was comforting for the children and me, but soul-destroying at the same time. In the last few months, I'd begun to instigate small changes, making the house more ours. The three of us were a new kind of family, and it was important we had a fresh start.

I sat in the tall chair and placed the coffee to one side, then considered the project I was working on. It was a pet portrait of a poodle, based on the hundred or so photos that the doting owners had sent me after their little Freddie had gone for his last walk over the rainbow bridge. Twenty or so of the photos were pinned along the side and top of my drafting table, and I sipped my drink as I checked them out. So many of them were perfect for a standard portrait, Freddie was an adorable canine, with bright black eyes and the curliest apricot fur. Not brown, that fact was underlined with great insistence, Freddie was an apricot miniature poodle, and when Mrs. Winters had handed over the photos she'd begun to cry.

The sheet was empty in front of me, and I'd lacked inspiration for what to do when I'd sat down yesterday. Instead, I'd worked on some simple preliminary sketches, looking for scale and it was these I laid out in front of me. The first was Freddie sitting like the cutest dog on the planet, with a Santa hat on his head. The next playing with his furry butt in the air, his front legs on the ground, his mouth wide in a puppy-grin, and the last was a professional shot of Mrs. Winters holding Freddie. There was so much love in that photo, and I moved the three sketches around, to select one when it hit me. What this dog deserved, what the owners needed, was for me to capture all of it somehow. I sorted some more, and then with the idea solid in my thoughts, I began to sketch. I missed lunch as usual, because when I'm drawing nothing else intrudes. It was the only balanced time I had, and I hoarded it jealously.

My phone rang twice, and both times my chest tightened when I thought it might be Eric. It wasn't either time, and I didn't know whether to be happy or miserable — *the story of my life.*

"Stow the self-pity, McMillan."

The first interruption was college. My contact there, Brooke Owens, checking up on the semester schedule she'd proposed. I couldn't ignore the call, because I'd made a commitment, and despite my social anxiety, I had to do this. Every semester I assisted, remotely, with end-of-term project work in the college marketing course.

It was all Spencer's fault that I'd even begun talking to the head of the art department at the college. After all, it had been him who'd suggested I get out of the damn house and hooked me up. Then when Paisley used her therapist-voodoo-magic on me, I'd found myself agreeing that maybe I could get out of the house if I could work on something I felt confident in. The art department needed someone to support a module on graphic art, not teach it, but mentor a few kids who loved the concept of creating graphic novels, and they needed me to be there face-to-face.

The therapy I'd done with Paisley so far, added to Spencer's encouragement, had been enough to help me attend Ash's wedding, and she was confident I could do more.

So I couldn't ignore this call, I had to talk to this Brooke woman, and maybe if I agreed to work at the college, then this might be a step to me becoming a different man. I could only hope that something changed in my life.

"Hi, Brady, this is Brooke. We have four students interested in the project, would Tuesday and Friday mornings work?"

No. I want to stay at home.

"Yes," I heard myself say.

"That's wonderful news, I'll email you the schedule, and I want to repeat what an honor it is to have you supporting our students. Your work is an inspiration to them, and I know they will get so much out of it."

"Thank you," because what else could I say? After the call ended, I wanted to phone her back and tell her that I'll probably only last one session, if I even made it to that. Glancing at the sketches of someone's pet, I sighed. How could a hermit with a paintbrush inspire any art student?

The second call was from my agent. I ignored that one because he wanted more from me, things that sold, graphic novels that meant something. I'd email him—emailing was me staying in my comfort zone as long as the speech to text worked okay.

I was so lost in concentration on composing the drafts that the ringing of the doorbell startled me, and I padded to the front door with my heart beating overtime. I couldn't be irritable because I assumed it was Ben, our local delivery driver who was making this week's art supply run. Ordering materials was my go-to when I was stressed, and even though it had been a few days since the wedding, I was still not quite over the mess in my head and had ordered ten different blues, all inspired I think, by the blue of Eric's eyes.

And, that was me, messed-up and weird over one kiss, and buying paints based on the eye color of a man who kissed like there was no tomorrow.

I opened the door expecting Ben the delivery driver, short, young, and sweet, and got Eric, tall, broad, and sexy.

"Hey," Eric offered with a grin. I peered past him to the drive, expecting Ash, even though I knew he was on his honeymoon.

"What happened?" I snapped. There could only be one

reason for Eric to be here, and it was to deliver bad news. *Then why is he smiling, idiot?*

"Huh," Eric followed my gaze to the big black truck sitting in my usually empty drive. "Nothing's wrong."

"Is Ash okay? Mia? Is it Sean?" Horror swept over me, at memories of another time when someone came to the door to explain my sister was dead. I staggered back, and Eric was there, right there, gripping my arm.

"Everything's good, Brady. They're having a wonderful time."

"Then, why are you here?"

He frowned as if I should find it obvious. "To see you, of course."

I shook off his hold and stepped farther back into my cool house. The initial panic subsided and then concern filtered in.

"You should have called me. I asked Sean to tell you to call me." Betrayal was bitter in my mouth.

"He did tell me," Eric said immediately. "This is all me, I'm sorry, but I was in the neighborhood." He had the grace to be embarrassed as I unpicked his sentence.

"In the neighborhood? Yeah right," I didn't believe a word he was saying. He looked so good though, big and sexy, and all the sensory memory of our kiss flooded back. "Why are you here? Why did you ask for my address? What do you want?" I stopped myself from adding more questions as he didn't interrupt me to answer any so far.

"Can I come in?" he asked after a moment's pause.

"Why?"

"You ask that a lot," he pushed his hands into the

pockets of his cut-offs. "But mostly I'm here because I owe you an apology and... look... can I come in?"

I was confused and thrilled that Eric was at my door. Even if how he'd found me was crossing a line, and he said he was here to apologize, which was a non-reason.

"I guess." I gestured into the hall, then headed to the kitchen, seeking safety with the coffee pot, and assuming he would follow, which he did. I chanced a look at him, and nearly swallowed my tongue, he was everything I'd ever liked in a man, the center of all my fantasies, and he was here alive and huge in my kitchen. I doubted I could've circled my hands around his thighs, but he wasn't muscle-bound, just fit, and the T-shirt he was wearing, emblazoned with CALFIRE, was so form-fitting I could see every line of him. I was hard and finding it impossible to hold on to my concerns over why he was here and how he found me. "Coffee? Or something cold?"

"How about something hot?" he winked at me.

Winked!

At me.

I pulled two mugs out of the cupboard but wasn't sure what to say in response to what probably wasn't a request for coffee. But which might have been, so I needed to stay calm and not read things into the situation.

Coffee done, I turned to face him, but he was a little too close. I had my bubble of space, and no one other than the kids were allowed inside that space without my agreement. As if he sensed my response, he moved back, and then he hunched. I wondered if he found it hard to stay out of people's personal space because of his size.

"You apologized at the wedding," I said, and couldn't

help but notice the hair on his chest, visible where the V of the T-shirt sat. I glanced down, and down, and then back up, meeting his heated gaze and swallowing.

"I wanted to explain as well, about Ash. Look, it's true that Ash asked me to look out for you. Only because, I think, the families are big and sprawling, I mean Leo's family is huge, and some of them were there, loud and in-your-face. Also, his aunt was there, the one in the purple hat and she has something nasty to say about everyone. Anyway, Ash wasn't trying to hook us up."

"Okay."

"So I said yes, that I would check in with you, and I looked over at you, and I knew it wouldn't be a chore, and then we chatted, and then you kissed me."

"Do you want me to say sorry for that again?" Was that what we were going to do? Spend all day apologizing to each other?

"God no," Eric let out a huff and opened up his hands holding them palm up. "I thought I'd like to do it again."

My mouth fell open, and I also nearly dropped my coffee. I placed it carefully on the surface because concentrating on what Eric was saying while carrying hot liquid was a recipe for disaster. Eric took another step away from me, giving me even more space, and then he tilted his head and hunched down even more.

Was he making himself look smaller? For me? Did he feel I'd be intimidated?

I wasn't daunted at all. I was shocked, turned on, and speechless, but nothing about Eric scared me.

"You don't need to do that," I blurted, and he frowned. Did that mean I'd insulted him or confused him?

"What?"

"Leaning over, I like it that you're tall and big, and… yeah."

He hesitated a moment then straightened up from the weird hunched thing he had going on. I'd never seen anyone that made me feel like I was burning from the inside out.

"Brady?"

I stepped closer to him. On my terms, I extended an invitation for him to join me in my personal space. "Yes?"

He moved. I moved.

And it was an inferno.

ELEVEN

Eric

I LIFTED HIM, or he climbed me, I didn't know what we were doing, all I knew for sure was that I had my hands under his ass, and somehow he was wrapped around me, and I backed him up to the work surface so I could go hands-free. This was fire and need, and the way he opened his mouth to me, the taste of him, the sounds he was making, I was surprised I hadn't come in my pants already. When I'd decided to visit, it hadn't been to scratch an itch. In my mind, today would've been talking, and learning, and soft, and quiet, and falling into that space that was a mutual attraction.

What I had instead was arms full of lust, and heaven help me, I didn't want to stop. He was faster and burned brighter than any fire that I'd been sent to extinguish, and I couldn't get enough. He scooted back and spread his legs, yanking me close, and taking what he wanted. I was so used to partners wanting me to push them, and hold them, that this wildfire was enough to have me yank myself away. I couldn't believe what I had here, what he wanted to do, and how confident he was. How could he want me?

"What?" he asked, his lips puffy from kisses, his skin flushed, and his eyes heavy with desire.

"I just... we..."

That appeared to be enough as he laced his hands behind my head and tugged me toward him, and then I didn't have the chance to speak again.

"Do you need me to do something?" I asked between kisses. Lovers always needed me to be strong for them, in charge, and I wanted to do this right.

"I need you to stay right here," he dived in for more. I groaned into the kiss and tightened my hold. The power he had now, the fact that he could make me moan with need was a heady feeling.

"Tell me what to do," I admitted, and cradled his face again, anything to make him see that I wanted to be told. He paused a moment and searched my expression, and I closed my eyes because I'd never felt so raw. "Please."

He stared at me for the longest time as if I was making no sense at all, and then he nodded.

"Undo your shorts," he demanded, "let me get my hands on you." I fumbled with my shorts, and all too quickly he had a handful of my ass, his fingers pressing at my crack, and I nearly freaking lost it there and then. "Undo mine," he said.

I lifted his ass to release him from his shorts. I was tall enough that sitting here when he spread his legs, I could step between them and we were at the same height, and the touch of his hard cock against mine was like coming home. Everything felt so right, perfect. I circled him and gripped as he fumbled for me and then groaned again. The kisses grew lazy, nothing more than exchanging muttered encouragement, and he kept telling me what he needed.

Touch me, kiss me, hold me, fuck me.

"Fuck, I want to be inside you," he muttered against my lips, he sounded wrecked but hopeful, and I wasn't going to hold back.

"Yes," I said, not leaving any room for doubt.

"You want me to tell you what I'm gonna do?" he asked, and I nodded, "I'm gonna get you on all fours and lube you up, and I'm going to fuck you so hard and hold you on the edge, and you're going to beg me to push—"

I had to stop him talking with a punishing kiss, and then my orgasm hit me hard, and even as I was coming, I knew I wanted to taste him and licked my way down to his belly and closed my mouth over the head of his cock. It was such a quick move I think he was surprised, but it was enough to send him over the edge, and he pushed my head away as he lost it hot and hard over my hand.

He buried his face in my neck, and held me so tight I wondered if he would ever let go.

"What did I do?" I thought I heard him murmur, and I could sense this going south fast. So I did what every good firefighter did, I went straight for the heart of the fire.

"That was fucking amazing," I said, and eased myself away a little, wincing as his hand left my biceps and shot out to grab kitchen paper towels. He wiped us down, used so much of it that I wondered if we'd need another roll of the stuff, and through all of it he wouldn't look up. Then he pulled down my shirt from where it was tucked up in my armpits and smoothed it. Only after he patted my chest did he glance up. I was losing him here, I could see that, his eyes darting everywhere but focusing on me.

"Look at me," I said with authority, and finally he met my gaze. Not for long but enough for me to see the uncertainty in the hazel-green depths of his eyes. "That was the hottest, sexiest, most in-my-face blaze I have ever faced." Okay, so some of that didn't make sense. Forest fires aren't sexy. Beautiful, deadly, yes, sexy no, whatever Frankie liked to think. "You telling me what you wanted to do, fuck, we need to do that again."

He bit his lip, seemed to be having a hundred conversations in his head, and then he buried his face back in my neck.

So much for talking.

TWELVE

Brady

WHAT DID I JUST DO?

The facts were black and white. I'd jumped his bones. Again. Only this time it had gone past kissing and straight on through to mutual orgasms, because once I'd had the feel of him in my hands, I couldn't stop. Not that he'd wanted to stop either, and he could have done at any minute, I hadn't been holding him in place.

Apart from the moment when I'd linked my hands behind his head and hadn't let him go, which was why I had my face buried right in that warm space where his neck and shoulder met. He smelled of sunshine and citrus, he was strong and steady, and I wanted more of that.

"Look at me," he repeated, "Brady, come on, look at me."

With my heart beating frantically in my chest, I finally moved back and glanced up, and he was smiling.

"Do I owe you an apology?" I asked, because if I did, then I wanted to get it out of the way before he left and I died of mortification alone in my painting space.

"For what?" He was confused. "The fastest, hardest orgasm I've experienced since I was fourteen and had my first blowjob? Or the fact that your kisses taste like nothing I've ever had before, and that I'm in danger of becoming addicted?"

"Me too," I said, "to all of it. Apart from the blowjob, I mean I was twenty-three. I need to shut up now."

He cradled my face with his hands, and I melted. "All I want is for you to promise me we can do this again."

"There are things you need to understand about me," I began, and swallowed hard. "I'm not an easy person to be around."

"Then you can tell me all about it when we have our first date."

"Date?"

"You think I'd have a taste of what it could be like with you and leave it at one orgasm?"

Oh, so not a real date, just orgasms then.

"But I had a tight hold of you." Was I looking for a reason for him to leave? When what I really wanted was to grab hold and not let go? I should've stopped talking, and just enjoyed the fact that my sex drought was over. "I was bossy and demanding—"

"And I fucking love that. I could have stopped you at any time." He kissed me on the forehead, then he picked me up, damsel-style, from the counter and carried me to the other side of the kitchen, depositing me by the fridge. That was some display of just how much he could handle.

"Oh," I said, and he laughed again, but it wasn't a mean laugh, it was happiness and sexiness all rolled into one.

"You called the shots. You didn't let me—fuck—that was so hot. So, a date?"

I concentrated on his words and ignored the fact that my right leg was twitchy and my arms ached like a bitch. "I have the kids," I said.

He checked around us, then placed his hands flat on the surface, caging me, and kissing me again. "I don't see them here."

"They're at school," I said, and he should've known that, right?

"I know," he said with exaggerated patience. "My point exactly."

"Oh, yeah, duh." *Oh god, now I sound like Lucas.*

"So, we're going to set a date. I'll text you my next clear day off?"

"I still want you to know what you're getting yourself in for."

His kisses deepened, he grabbed the remains of the paper roll, and in a smooth lift he took me from the kitchen to the couch, stumbling a little, but then I wasn't a lightweight, and depositing me on the sofa in my light-filled front room. This was surreal, this was a dream made real, and when he went to his knees in between my spread legs, I think I let out an unmanly squeak. Was he going to… Did he…?

Easing my shorts down, he stared at my cock which had gone past trying to harden to iron. How was this happening? Twenty-eight was a long way past fourteen, and my recovery rate was marred by the fact I usually fell asleep after getting myself off. I was already boneless, and he wanted to take more. He made a small noise of appreciation, then pressed his hands to my hips, and sucked my cock.

It took longer, but he didn't care. A couple of times I wanted to pull him up to kiss, admit I wasn't going to get off again, and then he swallowed deeper, one hand slipping up the length of me, the other caressing my balls, and every so often traveling to press against my hole. I wanted him there as well. I wanted everything, and I buried my hands in his hair, holding him tight, still, until that very last moment when I yanked at his hair, so he released me, and I was coming again.

Like a fucking teenager.

"I can't get enough of you," he said, getting himself off, as he kissed me again, finally stiffening and kissing me all at the same time, breathing through his orgasm right there into me. "All the kisses, all the time." I wasn't going to argue. He wiped us, and moved then, coming to sit next to me on the couch, then he put his arm around my shoulders and held me close. "So the date. I mean, I can keep doing that until you say yes."

"I already said yes, I wanted you to know why you might not want to."

"Nothing you say will change my mind," he squeezed me briefly, and I near-whimpered at the pleasure of being held so tight. I might've been aggressive when I knew what I wanted, but being cocooned like this was bliss. Ruining it wasn't my intention, but I may as well lay it all out there, and then maybe just beg when he decided to leave.

Old ghosts chased me, and uncertainty gripped me hard.

"I have Developmental Coordination Disorder," I paused for dramatic effect because at this point people stared at me or else asked me a stupid question. He did nothing, so I went for my next line of defense. "DCD as those in the trade like to call it." I laughed, without humor, and waited for the questions. The last guy I'd had this close had asked me if it was catching, which was *precisely* the intellectual level of guy I appeared to attract.

"How does it affect you?" he asked instead as if he understood something of what I was trying to say. Physically. Emotionally. Where did I start? *Probably with the stuff that he'll understand.*

"It's a lack of coordination between my mental intentions and my ability to carry out those intentions." There, I gave him the encyclopedia version of why I was different.

He mulled it over for a while. "Okay, like your brain knows how to tie laces, but maybe your hands can't follow your brain's instructions?"

"Yeah, that's exactly it. I've had occupational therapy to help me with most things, and after all these years I can fake most of it. I'm pretty clumsy, you've seen that. I don't drive. I never learned, and I don't want to. My muscles can get twitchy, but that might not be the DCD, who knows, and I have trouble reading people's expressions sometimes. Also, my memory is for shit on the best day, and reading is… hard. I didn't go to college, I struggled at school, I have dyslexia as well, but hey, it could be worse."

I ended my rehearsed speech on a hopeful note and found myself channeling my mom's words. *It could be worse, sweetheart.* That was what I wanted him to take away because he was going to leave now. That was how it went, me freaking out, plus me having kids, plus my memory, and my crippling insecurities and anxieties meant I made a shit boyfriend.

"It could be," he used a finger to tilt my chin. "You could be dying. That's worse."

"I have anxieties too, and I am never spontaneous outside of my comfort zone," I blurted, because hell, if I was chasing Eric away, then I was doing it properly.

"You plan everything?" Eric asked.

"Work out worst-case scenarios, yeah."

"But you let me in the door, and that was spur-of-the-moment, and then you kissed me, that was pretty impulsive as well."

I didn't know what he was getting at. Was he saying that I was lying about how much I think about the things that can go wrong? "I didn't have time to think," I defended.

"Maybe something about me stops you thinking?" Eric sounded as if he was contemplating his role in my impulsive action, and I didn't know what to say to that.

"Maybe you didn't trigger me," I decided. "I've learned how to identify the causes, I meditate, do yoga, I spend a lot of time gardening, and I question my thought patterns on a minute-by-minute basis. I've never had a partner that lasted longer than a month, so I got used to just being on my own, which means I'm not a good prospect. You see that, right?"

"Okay. Do you tell all of this to any guy you meet?"

"No, of course not."

He cradled my face and smiled. "Then I must be at least a little bit special, right?"

I hadn't thought of it that way. Most of the guys I'd been with just thought I was odd, and I never told them a single thing the same as I'd told Eric. So that was different. I nodded, because whatever he said I would still worry, and dissect, and stress over, but he didn't need to know that.

"When are the children home?"

I glanced at the clock. "An hour."

"So what about that date?" he asked again. "We have so much to talk about."

"I don't drive."

"I do. I like driving, and I have a truck that has a perfectly good passenger seat."

"But I have kids."

"I like kids."

"No I mean, I *have kids*. Responsibilities."

"Doesn't mean all of that gets in the way of sex."

Relief at the him-wanting-sex part switched immediately to disappointment. Sex. It was just sex. I could do that—fit it in around Lucas and Maddie, during the day when they were at school, and then hope flared in me that Eric would want to do that. With me. Even if an end date had already been set.

"Anyway," Eric continued, "when I meet the kids for real, it will be because us *together* has grown to mean something."

I sat upright and away from him. "What?"

"I would want them to know we were together."

"But... what if it's just sex?"

He pressed a hand to my cheek, "With me, I don't do 'just sex'. Does that scare you?"

"A little." I had to be honest with him because I was scared of a lot of things.

"I'm convinced it's going to be more, what can I say?" He stretched then, and his T-shirt rode up to give me a flash of his flat stomach, and the treasure trail that headed south. I wanted to touch, and from the way, he grasped my hand and placed it on his warm skin, I think I may have said that out loud. He released his hold, and I smoothed my fingers over his belly, stopping at a ridge of scarring, and lost in thought I bent over and kissed him there.

"What is that from?"

"Structure fire," he curled a hand in my hair.

"Like a house?"

"Office buildings."

"I thought you fought fires in the hills."

"Mainly I do, but we're also called out to support other teams in the city. Fires, traffic accidents, lost kids."

"So, what happened? Did you get trapped or something?"

"Propane tank exploded, I was in the way." He encouraged me up for another drugging kiss.

"Did it hurt? When it happened, I mean?" That was possibly the crassest question I'd ever asked, and I waited for him to shut down.

Instead, he took my hand and pushed it higher on his chest. "This one hurt more," he said, as I traced the rough skin. I didn't know if I wanted to hear the story if it was worse than an exploding propane tank.

"I lived in this… place… and Leo and Sean were close

by, at the end of the road by the trees, and I got talking, and we were all puffed up with who could dare whom to do what."

I glanced up at his face, he lived in a *place*? I should've asked him about that, but promptly forgot when he continued talking.

"So, Leo dared me to pedal downhill as fast as we could on our bikes toward a wall and see who stopped closest to the wall. I won the game, but the wall at the bottom didn't move out of the way." He chuckled. "The worst thing about it? Being cooped up inside with a broken arm for three weeks of summer." Then he sobered, and pressed his hand over mine, right where his heart was. "Back to now, though, I have things to say as well, things that make being with me difficult. As a first responder I could *see* worse, I could *be there* for worse, and anyone who is with me has to deal with that."

He was asking me if I could accept him for what he was. And, obliquely, he'd told me that he accepted me for who I was. Some of it went unspoken, but it was what I knew in my heart.

"I would worry about you every time you walked out the door, but I could work on it if we... if I had to."

He was asking for me to accept a much deeper connection than was warranted after one explosive hook-up, and I was suddenly wary. Was I actually contemplating seeing Eric again, and worse than that, considering something more than sex?

He huffed a laugh, "See how we both think we have things that make us loners? I'm going now, but I'll text you when I can next get over here, is that okay?"

"Yeah, I think... yeah."

He kissed me goodbye and left with ten minutes to spare, the kids trampling in, all loud noise and confusion, and it was as if he'd never been there at all.

The only evidence was the mugs we'd used, the missing kitchen roll, and somehow that didn't seem enough. I pressed fingers to my lips and recalled the kisses and the two orgasms that had left me feeling like jelly. Next time we met up on one of these *dates* he was mentioning I resolved that we'd talk first. I wanted to know more about him. I wanted to ask him when he'd started to go gray, and did he like peanut butter and jelly sandwiches, and what was his taste in music and movies, and did he have a big family.

I didn't want it just to be sex. I wanted him to see me as I was and think I was what he needed in his life.

"You look weird." Maddie's observation pulled me from my thoughts.

"Are you okay?" Lucas added, and poked me in the side. "You look all funny."

So I poked him back, and then Maddie. "You're the ones who are weird and funny." For a second, I waited for them to react badly. But Lucas laughed, and Maddie pushed me, and everything was right in my world.

And next time Eric was there, we were going to start again and do things right.

Even if the thought of holding back on mutual orgasms was a disappointing one.

THIRTEEN

Eric

I WISHED I had more time to think about Brady, but when I left that day and headed to shift, it was too busy even to talk, let alone think. Crazy hundred-plus temperatures had sent the city into madness, and by the time we were close to the end of the shift, we were all on edge and weary.

The fact that Ash Facetimed as I sat in the locker room after my shower was just the icing on the cake. I moved into the small anteroom for privacy and connected the call. Ash and Sean were happy, and smiled a lot, and explained how being in love and married was the best thing ever, and it was the kind of thing I wanted right now.

"Then we went paragliding," Ash announced, "although when we got there, the last guy landed and had a heart attack, and the leader asked if anyone was a doctor, and you'll never guess what happened."

"Sean saved him with a kiss," I deadpanned.

"Haha, no, Sean is a hero," Ash said and did this whole eyelash fluttering thing with his hands clasped to his chest.

"It was just a panic attack," Sean said dryly and pressed a kiss to Ash's cheek.

"Oh, look who's awake," Ash said and disappeared from view. Back when they'd planned this honeymoon to Myrtle Beach, they'd contemplated letting Ash's sister, Siobhan, take Mia for the week. That plan had lasted only one minute, maybe less. The suite they had was right on the beach, with a separate room for Mia. A brightly colored blow-up dinosaur, clearly Mia's, lurked behind them. In fact, the two of them had spent more time organizing things for Mia than they had for themselves.

Ash came back in view, and with him, Mia, looking sleepy, her lips pouty and her wayward curls sticking up all over the place.

"Hey Mia," I waved at the screen.

"Nen Nen," she babbled and reached for the phone, which Sean moved just in time. They all disappeared for a second when all I could hear was Mia repeating Nen Nen, which was what she said instead of Eric, at least we all thought that was what she was saying. I was running with it because she'd said that before she got anywhere with the name Leo.

"I've seen the news," Sean murmured when Ash disappeared with Mia who was babbling excitedly about something. "The fire…"

"Yeah."

A hundred things passed between us, the same as usual. Stay safe. Come home. Do the right things. Save lives. It had gotten to the point that fires in the brush around the city were more commonplace than they used to be, meaning we had a year-round threat to watch for. The fire might have been under control, but it was just one of many that threatened to become more. I was tired, and I didn't want the conversation to go that way.

"Married life looks good on you," I said instead.

He took the subject change and ran with it. "I kind of like it." His head jerked, and he rubbed at it, looking back at where I assume Ash had reminded him he was right there, with a slap upside his head. "I love it, and I love you," he called out.

"Your turn to change Mia," was the reply. With some good-natured huffing, Sean passed the phone to Ash with a waved, later.

"I wanted to ask about Brady," Ash said, quickly, as if maybe that had been the whole reason for the call.

"What about him?" I tried to sound as calm as I could, but just the mention of his name had me tense. I wasn't sure where I was with Brady, although he hadn't dismissed us meeting up again. I wanted to know everything about him, things like how did he handle being a dad and an uncle all wrapped up in one. And how the hell had he learned to kiss like nothing else in the world mattered?

"I need you to call him about what I said at the wedding," Ash began. "He wasn't happy about me asking you to look out for him, and I don't want him angry."

"I saw him today."

Ash's eyes widened. "You did? You texted him and he said it was okay for you to visit?"

"Kind of," I hedged. Then I took a deep breath. I shared everything with Leo and Sean, and by extension, Ash. They were best friends, but like brothers as well, and I was never very good at keeping secrets.

"I didn't text him I just went to visit him, and we kissed, and I'm one hundred percent certain that I will be seeing him again."

"You're what?" Sean asked from the background.

"Is that a problem?"

"Not with me, dude," Sean called, "it's a step up from Walmart-Yogurt-Guy."

I bit my tongue, even though I wanted to throw in a fuck you. Mia would not learn the word fuck from her Uncle Eric.

"Ash?" I prompted because he was quiet.

"Can you be careful?" was all he said.

I nodded. "Always."

"He's a good guy and has a heart of gold. I'm happy you've connected." He frowned again. "He wants this too, right? To see you, I mean."

"Yes."

"Okay then, good."

We said our goodbyes, and my last image was when Ash turned the phone to show me that Sean was changing a diaper with one hand and giving me the finger with the other.

With friends like that… I snorted a laugh and felt lighter.

"You coming over to Frankie's for a bit?" Gemma called from the door. She and Frankie were a thing, or at least I thought they were. I wouldn't ever say anything unless needed, a couple on a team could work against us, but I was watching closely. I didn't fuck about with safety, and if I sensed anything going down, then I would be the first to talk to them. Right now, they just seemed to be at the flirting-friends stage, and it wasn't affecting their reactions in the field. In fact, it was at the sweet-cute stage, and it warmed my heart to see affection growing in the face of the adversity we'd been facing.

We were all on standby, this meant a maximum twenty-four-hour downtime, but we knew it could be shorter, maybe closer to eight, and all five of the team lived close enough that we could get to the fires if needed.

Knowing it was only a matter of time.

FOURTEEN

Brady

THE NEXT TIME ERIC VISITED, we talked for all of ten minutes before we ended up in the bedroom. At first I thought we should talk, but actually I was happy with just sex. Not just the fact we exchanged mutual blowjobs and then ended up showering together, but that there wasn't too much time for discussions about anything meaningful except for negotiations about what position to get into, and how hard to suck.

He couldn't stay long, but he did see some of the art I'd pinned on the door of the closet.

"These are so cool," he murmured and traced the caricatures I'd done of the guests at the wedding, all from memory. He snorted when he spotted the final one. "Leo's Aunt Bridgette and that awful purple hat, you've captured her perfectly."

"Would you like to see some other stuff?"

He smirked at me. "I've seen quite a lot." Then he turned serious. "Yes, please."

I showed him the sketch of the apricot poodle that was half-finished and the pages of the graphic novel I was working on, and he made all the right noises, complimenting each one. Then he turned with interest to the other wall.

"Is this your work as well? It's all very different."

"No, those are all student projects that I assist with."

He sent me a surprised glance, one I'd expected. "You teach?"

"Not really. I mean, I mentor remotely, and sometimes the students come here if they need help, but mostly… no, not the college itself, although they want me to, but that would take a lot to get me there, help, inner strength, all that kind of thing."

Wow, I was being super honest here, and I didn't even know Eric that well. What was it that was telling me it was okay to share things with him? Was it his solemn eyes, or the gentle way he held me, or was it because the orgasms had melted my brain?

"You're an amazing man," he kissed me again. "And you're stronger than you think you are, I know it."

The third time he visited, we managed twenty minutes of talking, but that was my fault. He asked me what art I was working on, and I made the stupid mistake of telling him, which led to us spending too long in my small art nook and examining the new novel pages. I didn't want to talk about important things, I wanted more sex. I was addicted.

"You blow me away," he murmured, as he peered at the newest commission I was working on. He spotted that I'd finished the three poses of the dog. "Wow, that is so lifelike. Could you do something like this for Leo, of Cap, his dog, I mean?"

"Of course, I'd just need some photos to work from."

"Consider yourself commissioned." He went back to the page of art, and all I could think was that this was a tiny space for a huge man to be standing in. The area was filled with him, but not just physically, although that was a given. He smelled so good, and from the position I was in, standing in the doorway, I had a clear view of his back muscles, his ass, the way his shorts hugged his thighs, the rise of his CALFIRE T-shirt exposing flesh, and the dark hair on his legs. Even his goddamn feet were perfect. But it was more the gentle presence of him, the way he smiled at me and made me feel happy from the inside out. I knew it wouldn't last, that it wasn't going to be *more*, but I knew that the day he called it all off, or when I drove him away, I would miss his calming presence. Eric Lester made me feel as if I wasn't a clumsy person who lacked the skills to write, or who tripped over thin air. He made all those horrible messy parts that fought inside my head go still.

I felt as if I'd waited my entire life for him, and part of me thought about shutting the door and keeping him locked in my office. I laughed a little at that, and he turned to face me, his gorgeous face lit up with a smile.

"What?" he took the single step that would bring him closer to me.

"I just had this image of locking you in here to keep you," I blurted, before my brain fully engaged.

He wriggled his eyebrows and placed his hands on my shoulders, sliding them down to cup my elbows. "Would you stay in here with me?"

"It's a tight fit," I pretended to muse.

"You know I can beat down doors with my fists," he growled, and leered at me, before snorting a laugh at himself.

Heat curled and spat and hissed inside me, at the groan and the laugh, surging out in a desperate need to kiss him, desperate to climb this man as if I was never going to have sex again.

"Fuck me," I demanded, and moved away from him, going straight to the bedroom, crawling over the bed, nearly reaching my bedside cabinet, when he caught me from behind and tugged me to a stop, rolling me over and caging me under his hands.

"You're sure?" he asked, and a million questions sat in those quiet words.

Was I sure? God, if I didn't have that connection in the next five minutes, I might have to dig out porn and my ever-handy dildo. I wanted to be inside him, but this time, I needed him to take care of me. Fast.

He went up on his knees and eased down my shorts and boxers. I was embarrassingly hard, something I tried to cover, and God knows why I did that. He eased my hand aside, let out a low whistle of appreciation, and crouched over to spend way too long licking and sucking and fondling for my liking. It was as if he had four hands, he caressed my balls, pressed the tip of his finger to my hole, sucked on each ball, slipped his hand along the length of me, bit marks into the skin on my hips. All I could do was hold on for the ride. I curled my fingers into the quilt cover and tried not to whimper with need.

"Let me hear the words," he murmured, and tracked kisses up my body, easing my T-shirt over my head and drawing out a deep kiss.

"Huh?" I was dazed and stupid for more.

"What do you like?" he asked, nuzzling into my neck and kissing me there, trailing touches down to my nipples, pulling at them, rolling them in his fingers. "You like me touching you there?" I nodded, words long gone from my head, and he bent his head and sucked, then bit gently. The sharp prick of pain had me gasping.

He immediately stopped. "Too much?" he sounded concerned.

I could tell him it was, but I'd be lying. "Harder," I said, and he did exactly what I'd asked, the pain hardwired to my cock like I'd never experienced.

"What about here?" he asked when he had his fingers tracing patterns on my balls, under them to my hole. "You like me sucking them?"

Fuck. Any more questions and I was going to come embarrassingly fast.

"In. Me," I demanded.

He gave my cock one final service, before standing and stripping his clothes. He was just as hard, wanted me as much as I wanted him. "Where is the stuff?" he asked, and caged me again, leaning over me to my drawer. I waved in that general direction, and with dexterity he had a condom on and lube on his fingers in less time than I'd ever imagined. It took me forever to get a condom on, but practice and perseverance made me appear halfway competent.

Stop. Just stop thinking.

"How do you want me?" I asked.

He stopped what he was doing, and stared right at me, so close I could feel the puff of his breath on my face. "What do you want?"

I want everything. "I want to see you," I said, and coughed to clear my throat which was choked with emotion. Lovers I'd been with before hadn't asked what I wanted, they decided for me. It was the worst kind of insult that they'd all decided to take care of me. I wasn't needy, not in that way. I wanted equality and respect in the bedroom, togetherness, a feeling of it being fifty-percent him, and fifty me.

"You don't know..." He kissed me and shuffled up the bed a little, his muscular thighs giving me support, "...how turned on you make me saying things like that."

He talked a lot during sex for a quiet man, with every kiss he told me he wanted me, saying how sexy I was, how this was everything. I believed it all because every word was mirrored in firm but achingly tender touches, with kisses so hot I was burning up.

He ran a finger over my hole, and the slick was enough to make it glide, before he pressed the tip in, and I swallowed my groan. I craved the pleasure-pain of this and allowed myself to relax, and still he kissed me as he worked to loosen me, with so much lube and laughter that before I knew it he was there, and after the initial pause when my body adjusted, he was in.

He rocked slowly, kissing, talking, my cock trapped against my belly, my hands held still in his, and I was losing my fucking mind.

"You're so beautiful," he muttered, and kissed each eyelid, the tip of my nose, sucked at my neck, the point of my chin, then back to my lips. Then he angled the press of him inside me, took one of my trapped hands, and pushed it between us. "Touch yourself," he said, or whimpered, nothing sounded the same right then.

I eased my hand farther in, the tips of my fingers brushing my cock, moaning at the sensation, but not wanting to finish yet, sliding my hand up, tenderly following the curls of hair there, and tweaking at his nipples. I swear his eyes rolled into the back of his head, and he whimpered, and I'd found his kryptonite. He liked it hard, I twisted and caressed, and even tried in vain to get my lips to them, but with a groan, he hunched even more.

"I'm close," he warned, "Brady…"

I wanted to come just from my cock being trapped, and instead of reaching for myself, I used my free hand to grip his ass as best I could, grind closer, and it was seconds before my orgasm exploded, every part of my body shaking with it, my eyes closing as I arched up into him.

"Open your eyes, Brady, open them," he pleaded, and when I did, he was staring into my soul, and when his orgasm hit he kissed me hard, and I fell for him in an instant.

The next few times he arrived there was some talking,

laughter as we fucked, a few casual questions about my art, or his CALFIRE team, but we'd gotten into the routine of jumping each other as soon as he arrived.

Almost like anonymous sex, and *just* what I wanted.

Right?

FIFTEEN

Eric

"CAN WE TALK?" Dale cornered me in the locker room, and I tightened my towel around my waist. Our team leader had this annoying habit of trying to have serious conversations right after showers.

"Can I dress first, sir?" I asked, and waited as he mulled it over.

"Come find me," he agreed after that hesitation and then moved away.

I was dressed and ready to go within ten minutes and found him pacing the technical room, from one end to the other. This wasn't a good sign, because he only paced when something was wrong.

I waited until he'd turned to face my way. "Lieutenant?"

"Oh, shut the door, Eric, will you?"

This sounded serious, and it worried me that the rest of the team weren't there. Parker was in the office, I'd just passed him, and Gemma and Frankie had car-shared, a euphemism for God knows what.

"It's a delicate situation," he began, and I tensed. I knew what the issue was immediately. "Have you noticed that Gemma and Frankie are…"

"Yes." I wasn't going to prevaricate when this was a serious issue.

"So it's not just me?"

"No."

He sank to the nearest chair and let out a string of curses. Finally, he looked up at me, "I'm happy for them but, shit, Eric."

I turned a chair and straddled it opposite him, then waited for him to elaborate.

"I need to talk to them, work out what we're doing here. They're both good, I don't want to lose either of them, but if there was any implication that the team was compromised? Okay, thank you, Eric, for your honesty. Get some sleep. We're back in twenty-four."

Unless it all goes to shit.

I rationalized heading north to Brady's place because I could sleep there if I needed to, after we spent a long time kissing, and maybe it could be him fucking me. I stopped off at home first, loaded Cap into the car, as it had been my turn to have him, with Leo off training this week and Sean still on his honeymoon. We had a dog walker we could call on if we were all on duty at the same time, but that had become less necessary with Ash working from home. Mia and Cap had become fast friends, and I loved watching them together. In fact, the last few days Cap had been subdued, as it seemed the humans weren't the only ones missing Mia. I paid the dog walker for the day, and she left with a smile, and then it was time to go.

When we arrived at Brady's, I realized I hadn't even asked if he liked dogs.

"Be good," I warned Cap, who stared at me with a goofy doggy grin and then proceeded to scratch his ear. "No barking, climbing, eating things you shouldn't, pooping on carpets, marking territory, eating decorative candles, or sleeping on the couch." He tilted his head as if he was actually listening. "Brady might not even like dogs, and I want to make a good impression. Are you with me here?" I held out a hand for a high five, and Cap offered his paw. "Okay, then."

I sent a quick text to Leo to tell him where I was , and then I clipped the leash on Cap before picking up the things I'd purchased at the store near our house. The wine was polite, the candy my weakness. As to the flowers I'd picked from Ash's front yard, well they were something of a statement. I couldn't say that I'd ever given another man flowers and maybe it wasn't appropriate, but when I'd seen the yellow blooms sitting there looking pretty, I had to pick them. I was sure that Ash wouldn't notice the hole in the plant where they'd once been. I'd blame Cap if worse came to worse.

Juggling everything, and with Cap tugging at his leash, I realized I was a whole mess of everything landing on Brady's doorstep. I should have texted him to tell him I was coming over. He might not have been in, but I knocked anyway.

He answered and stood in the doorway, not precisely welcoming me with open arms.

"Lucas is home sick," he inclined his head to a spot behind him.

Did that mean Brady wanted me to go? We hadn't had a conversation about talking to the kids. But I wanted to, only if Lucas was ill, and Brady was in carer mode, then maybe today wasn't the right moment? I lowered my voice, "Did you want me to go?" God, how I wanted him to tell me to stay, but I could see the hesitation in his expression, only he never got a chance to say a word.

"Hey," Lucas said from behind him. "Is that your dog?" he asked and went to his knees. I relaxed my hold on the leash, and Cap took all the affection he was given.

"I can go," I said, but something in Brady's expression stopped me. He was staring down at Lucas, and his mouth had fallen open.

His attention snapped back to me. "No, please come in. I have coffee." He moved to one side to let me in, and I thrust the sunshine-colored flowers at him.

"For you," I announced, then handed over the Haribo and the wine as well. He looked overwhelmed for an instant, and then he made his way to the counter and placed everything down gently. I shut the door and unclipped Cap's leash, which was the signal that he could fall on his back and expose his belly for rubs. Lucas was laughing, roughhousing, and I veered into the kitchen.

"Lucas seems okay," I said and knew I'd approached it the right way when Brady closed his eyes briefly.

"Yeah," was all he said. He then concentrated on coffee, and now that I knew he had DCD, and after I'd done a shit ton of research in every spare second, I could see how everything he did had that quiet deliberation. Nothing was rushed or spilled, and it was as if he was counting down the steps in his head.

"Can I do anything?" I asked, forever the polite guy. The reason I bought gifts was the same reason I asked to help—ingrained into me by a momma who was all about society and niceties. Today I'd decided that we weren't going straight to the mutual masturbation, but were actually going to learn more about each other. Not that Brady knew that of course.

"Can I take Cap to the yard? We have a ball," Lucas asked. "I can get him a bowl of water, and we'll stay in the shade." He was asking me as if I was the one who could give permission.

"If your uncle says it's okay," I said and deferred to Brady.

"How are you feeling?" Brady asked Lucas with a serious expression on his face.

"Better," Lucas murmured, but couldn't quite meet Brady's gaze. Then as in an afterthought, he pressed a hand to his belly. "Still a bit sick," he added. I could tell he was lying, Brady had to be able to tell he was, too.

"Be careful of the pittosporum, I only just cut them back, and if you feel sick come back indoors," Brady said.

Lucas, laughing like a loon, along with a whining, excited Cap, went to the back door, but as an afterthought, he came back to Brady and hugged him, then vanished out through the kitchen door and into the yard. As soon as the door shut, Brady leaned heavily on the work surface and sighed.

"He seems better," I said, cautiously.

"We all know that he isn't sick."

"He's faking?"

"Yep. It's career day at school, they have parents

visiting, and he didn't want to go because that would mean me being there. He thinks I don't know about the day, but I saw the letter, and I do. He woke up this morning and told me his belly ached, and I didn't push it." Brady shook his head. "It's a long story."

I imagined that having lost his mom and dad, it would be hard on a day specifically targeted on showcasing parents.

"Did you not want to go in for him instead, I mean, you're the one raising them now?" I stepped a little closer to Brady, touching his arm gently.

"He didn't ask me." Brady moved away, and I took that as a sign he didn't want to be touched, so I dropped my hand and leaned on the opposite counter. "It's not about being an uncle even, I mean, Lucas has two best friends, one has an aunt who is an airline pilot, the other's aunt is a neurosurgeon, and they've gone in. I can't beat that, hell I'm not even sure what you would call my *career*. Or me, come to think of it. I'd probably fall over, or forget the words, or make an idiot of myself. He's protecting me is all."

Wow, there was a lot of loneliness and bitterness in that last comment, neither of which I'd seen in Brady before.

"You're an artist."

"Whatever, it's nothing to worry about, he'll go back tomorrow, and everything will be fine. Thank you for the wine and the Haribo. I should put this alstroemeria in water because otherwise, they'll last five minutes even with the AC on. Only, I guess AC tends to dry out the air, and that would make them die even quicker—"

I glanced out to check Lucas was preoccupied with

Cap and hauled Brady to face me and kissed him, interrupting the stream of thought about the flowers, before setting him away and rubbing his upper arms. "I've wanted to do that since you opened the door."

Brady was surprised at first, then he did his own check out of the door and pressed a quick kiss to my lips.

"Me too."

Picking up our coffees, I then gestured with my elbow in the direction that Lucas had run.

"How about you show me your yard?"

He stood still for a moment. "You honestly want to stay? Even though Lucas is here?"

This was dangerous, he seemed confounded, as if I was just there for sex, and of course, if Lucas hadn't been here then there would have been sex, but I also wanted to talk to Brady, get to know him and Lucas, and I wasn't ready to cut and run.

"You said it's your peaceful place, right? I want to see what kind of yard you have. Maybe talk about plants and things."

He was dubious, whether that was because of my declaration at having an interest in his plants, or that I wanted to stay, I didn't know. But I ignored him, and moved closer to the door, waiting for him to open it. When we were out on the small patio, I was faced with a very different backyard than the ones I was used to. This was big, with an intricate network of raised beds, filled with things that I never thought would have survived a San Diego summer, let alone be so healthy. We wandered around the space, narrowly missing flying tennis balls and one very hard Frisbee. Lucas had given up all pretense at being ill and was having the time of his life as was Cap who never got this much attention on a workday.

Brady gave me a guided tour around his backyard.

"These are Anigozanthos, or what you might know as Kangaroo Paw," Brady said and crouched by a sturdy red bush. "It's originally from Western Australia, and the flowers look like tiny kangaroo paws, see?" He supported one flower with a tender touch, and I leaned in as instructed, to examine it. I didn't know what a kangaroo paw was like, but these flowers had a foot-type arrangement. "I put it in front of the white wall because I thought it stands out," he finished with a shrug.

"It's stunning. Your place here, it's truly stunning."

He colored in embarrassment and leaned in to pick at something on the kangaroo bush, frowning at it and then stalking off to another part of the garden. "Snail," he explained as he returned and patted the sizeable red bush. Caring for things seemed to be second nature to him, and a strange warmth stole into me.

"You love your garden," I observed and rubbed his arm to reassure him that I was genuine because he appeared to need that.

"I do, I mean, see this Trachelospermum Jasminoides?" he lifted an offshoot of a bush with tiny star-shaped flowers. "Once I've seen a plant, I can recall its name. Ask me to write it down, and I'd be lost, but with a name I have everything. It's a flowering plant, obviously, and it's part of the Apocynaceae family, which is native to eastern and southeastern Asia. Here we call it the star jasmine, and it has to be well-drained, but it can tolerate some drought.

It's here in the full sun, but it will also grow and flower in partial shade."

"All I know is that it's white and gorgeous."

He smiled and went to a crouch which I copied, although his crouch was a lot more graceful than mine. "You have to mulch though to retain some moisture." He poked around the base of the bush and then seemingly satisfied, he stood and brushed himself off, then extended a hand to me. I could've ignored the hand because I was worried I'd pull him over, but I didn't.

"I volunteer with Leo and Sean at this place called Ringwood, it's a foster home, and we sometimes go to the gardens there. Not that the three of us know anything about gardening, but you could come with me one time and tell us what to do?"

God knows where that had all came from, and I regretted saying it because his eyes widened and he seemed squirrelly all of a sudden. Then, as if he was talking himself down, he let out a breath.

"Maybe, one day."

"Yeah, that would be great, because our garden is just bushes. None of us are gardeners."

"The wedding was beautiful," he said.

"We hired someone in, at least I think we did, Ash organized that."

He bit his lip. "Ash asked if I wanted to do it. I said no." Then he glanced up at me, and I didn't know what he was expecting me to say, but I hadn't planned on saying something crass like, he should have, or that he was silly not to have done.

"Trust me. You didn't want to be anywhere near Ash in groomzilla mode."

Brady smiled then, sharing the joke. "I was the one who talked him off the edge of the cliff the night before the wedding," he said, then frowned. "Not that he didn't want to get married, he was so happy and excited, he just wanted everything to be perfect for the day, and he has this tendency to overthink things."

"Ash and Sean are good together." I laced my fingers with his.

Like we could be good together.

"They are." Brady squeezed my hand, and I wanted to believe that he agreed with my unspoken assessment of us together. I wanted to stay there all day, drinking coffee, hearing more about his garden, and the snails, and the colorful purple and pink daylilies he said were just as beautiful as the traditional yellow and orange. He'd been so defensive of those vibrant flowers that I wanted to kiss him again even if Lucas had been staring at us expectantly.

"Are you his boyfriend?" Lucas asked me as Brady and I were inspecting the trachelosp-something-or-other growing over a wooden arch to form a canopy of fragrant shade. It was just an excuse to touch him, and he wasn't moving away, so I thought he was happy with it.

"Lucas," Brady warned.

I felt Brady stiffen next to me, and he unlaced his hand from mine. That was not a good sign, and I had no idea how Brady wanted to play this. Was *us* a secret? Was this more than sex based on an attraction that was hot as hell? I should've waited to see what Brady said, but I could see

Lucas' eyes narrowing, and he seemed to be waiting for an official statement.

"Yes," I blurted out and sent a chagrined look at Brady, who closed his eyes and rubbed at his temple. *Shit. I have overstepped hugely.*

"We're taking it slow," Brady murmured as he opened his eyes.

"Cool," Lucas said, and that was the matter settled. He had another question, and I braced myself for it. "And you're a firefighter, right?"

Oh. That was an easy question. "I am."

At that moment, which was fortunate, Cap bounded up with the Frisbee in his mouth and dropped it at my feet. On instinct, I picked it up and threw it, with dog and boy chasing it.

"You make that look easy. The last time I threw a Frisbee it landed on the roof. Actually, it's still up there as far as I'm aware."

"I could get it down for you?" My instinct was to show him how useful it was to have a *boyfriend* with access to ladders.

"It's okay, I got them another one, and I won't throw it again. I should be licensed to be able to handle a dangerous Frisbee."

I stole a quick kiss as he smiled at his joke. I mean, I could kiss him now that I'd told Lucas we were boyfriends, whatever that meant in this day and age. Maybe we should've talked about that, set some boundaries he was comfortable with, because I was well and truly smitten and caught in his snare.

"We should talk about the boyfriend thing," I began as I backed away.

"It's okay. I get it's what you had to say at the time." Brady smiled as if he believed that was what I actually meant.

"No, it's what I wanted to say, I like the label even if the cool kids don't use it anymore. There again, I was never one of the cool kids."

"Me neither."

"So, you want to go with it? Exclusive?" I moved closer to lower my voice. "Cuddle on the couch. Tell each other secrets? Hold hands?"

"Oh," he sounded surprised, then worried. "I haven't done that before."

How could he not have held hands and exchanged secrets? Why hadn't he had that in his life? I hated his doubt, and Lucas watching us be damned, I cradled Brady's face and kissed him, then I held his hand and tugged him into my side.

"There's a first for everything," I said, and he laced his fingers with mine again, the scent of the flowers around us, the shade cool, Lucas' laughter, and Cap's happy yips, just made everything a million times better. I didn't want to leave.

Which was precisely the moment my cell vibrated in my shorts. I had to look, but part of me didn't want to get yanked away from Brady standing in the riot of colors and scents.

"Sorry," I twisted to take my cell out with my free hand, glancing at the screen. "I need to go."

"You said you might have to."

"We're only back at the station. I'll get some sleep, nothing to worry about." I was all into the reassurance for my new *boyfriend*.

"I'm not worried," he kissed me one last time. "Stay safe."

I whistled for Cap, who jumped back into my truck. I waved at Brady and a mournful-looking Lucas, and drove to the station, messaging Leo to pick up Cap when his training was finished for the day. I was first there, and sleep was easy for the limited time we had, particularly when memories of kissing Brady chased me into my dreams.

SIXTEEN

Brady

I STAYED at the front door long after Eric's truck had disappeared around the bend. I'd just told him the biggest lie ever, that I wasn't worried. But I *was* worried, and not just because I knew he would be going off to fight a fire, but that we'd abruptly become *more* in the time he'd been here. He'd stayed even though we weren't going to have sex. He'd stayed to talk to me about normal things like my love for the garden and had also appeared interested in what I wanted to say.

I liked Eric. That was the crux of the matter. He had a shyness all of his very own, an uncertainty in him that I found endearing.

"Can we get a dog?" Lucas asked as soon as I shut the door.

"When you're older," I gave my standard reply. It wasn't fair on the kids, after all, I was home all day, but the idea of adding a dog into the chaotic mix in my head was too much to contemplate at the best of times.

Lucas sighed dramatically but didn't argue, gotta love him for that.

"Talking of older, we need to chat about a few things."

His eyes widened, and then he just appeared guilty. "Like what? When I'm older? Or you? What's wrong?"

"Let's go and sit on the couch."

"I don't want to," Lucas seemed shifty, and took a step backward toward the stairs. This was the moment he ran off, and he knew damn well I wouldn't follow him up to his room because I didn't do that. We had one rule in the house that our bedrooms were our safe, quiet places, more for my benefit than theirs I suppose, because sometimes I just needed to escape chaos and sit in silence.

"Then we'll do it here—"

"I have homework."

"I know you weren't ill today, I completely get why you don't want to do the family career event, but I want to reassure you that if you need more family counseling we can all go, or you can on your own, it's up to you." I was blunt and exactly to the point, and Lucas' eyes were wide, and then he grimaced. "You want to tell me why?"

"No, please don't ask me, and I don't want counseling," he grew mutinous, "I don't need to do any more talking, I'm grown up now, and I know what I'm doing." His hands were in fists, and he was bristling with tension. But grown up? At twelve?

"Lucas, come on—"

"I'm fine. Leave me alone."

And then he ran, and I was left standing there like an idiot. Not having a mom or dad to take in, or other aunts, uncles, left him with me. I didn't want to think that what

I'd said to Eric was right—that I had nothing to give to a class of children, nor did I have a glamorous career, and I wasn't a real dad.

But in my gut, that is what I held as truth.

When he came back down, it was apparent he'd been crying, and he was carrying his memory box which he placed on the counter as he clambered on to a kitchen stool. The kids had their own memory boxes, filled with all kinds of things I'd rescued the day I'd destroyed Nicole's closet. From concert tickets to photos, to the wedding invitation from Dan and Nicole's big day, there were different things in each box, and I had one of my own, filled with things that spoke of the fact my sister had also been my closest friend.

Mine was different in that the contents went a long way back, but I'd told the kids the stories connected to each, and one day everything would belong to Maddie and Lucas. There were photos of the two of us as kids, her with braces and pigtails, me with skinned knees and a goofy smile looking adoringly up at her, not to mention a copy of the reading book that she'd spent hours training me on until I could fake I was reading it. She knew how much it meant for me to have something that I could show Mom and Dad, to make them proud, to seem normal. Mom had cried the day I read it. Dad had patted my back in his usual gruff way. I couldn't think of my box right now, not when Lucas had been crying.

He removed the lid and peered into the depth of the box, pulling out menus, photos, and the one thing that meant everything to him, the hospital identity bracelet from when he was born.

"Can you tell me the story?"

I'd told him this so many times, but I loved telling it to him as much as he loved hearing it. "It was raining. I remember that, and we'd had the mother of all storms the night before, so your dad was over-prepared. He had ten different ways to get to the hospital in case of flooding, and he'd taken courses, just in case they were stuck somewhere. Your dad, he was always a soldier, organized, aware of everything, and he was beyond excited that you were coming. Your mom though, she just let him get on with it, absolutely calm, and the two of them together, they just wanted you."

"Tell me about Dad's car again."

I chuckled when I recalled Dan's car. "He had this beat-up Mustang, which I think had once been blue, although no one was entirely sure. He loved that car, and it ran like a dream, but he was so worried it would break down on the way to the hospital he traded it in for this brand-new Toyota. Your mom repurchased the Mustang for him when she found out and told him that when she was in labor, he could choose which car to take."

"But he didn't need to."

"Nope, they were at the hospital for a checkup, and you made an appearance two weeks early. I remember getting the call."

"Tell me what Dad said." This was both of our favorite part of the story.

"He cried, and laughed, and told me to get myself to Soledad Memorial, because the very best thing in his and your mom's lives had just appeared, and it was a miracle."

Lucas pulled out a tiny teddy, with a big spotted bow.

"And they gave this to me when Maddie was born, told me it was a present from her."

"They did."

He stared directly at me, and I waited for the next question. Instead, he wriggled on the stool and then gripped the teddy tight.

"It wasn't because I don't have a mom or dad that I didn't go in today, Uncle Brady." He dipped his gaze, and my chest was tight, I already knew where this was going. "I know they would want to see your pictures because they are the best ones in the entire world." He sounded so proud, and some of the tightness eased. "It's just not fair to make you go in when you don't want to. I don't want anyone to laugh at you because I would get suspended for hitting them."

And there it was. He *was* the grown-up, looking out for me, making my life easy, and seeing the path that my going to school could take. I could've stood up there, panicking, not recalling the words I wanted to say, maybe even falling over my own fucking feet. Hell, I even did parent-teacher meetings on Skype, but the school understood, and I had made it to the school on some occasions when it was quiet, and I could visit in peace, one-to-one. I wasn't housebound, not agoraphobic, but at home, I was safe, and Spencer helped with the things I couldn't manage. That was all.

"Okay," I began. "How about next time you tell me, and maybe I ask Spencer to come in with me to help."

"What if…?"

"If people laugh, then I will draw a cartoon with them doing something silly, so we can all laugh back." Okay, so that was probably a parenting fail, but fuck it, I refused to let Lucas be so worried on my behalf.

"For real?"

I reached over to clasp his hand, and he turned it so he could lace our fingers.

"Yes," I said. "For real."

"Cool," he shut the box. "Can you make me Mom's magic chicken soup?" He patted his belly and gave me a sly glance. "I *am* ill, you know."

I reached over and gave him the biggest noogie known to man, and he squealed and managed to get away, promising retribution and throwing water from his bottle at me. He was fine, not ill at all, and he'd been looking out for me. I loved him, and Maddie, so much it hurt, and just spending the day with my wayward nephew and listening to him talk made me feel l was doing something right.

And then, even though he wasn't actually ill, I made the soup.

I didn't see Eric for nearly a week. He'd had some kind of training course, and also three shifts that he told me were quiet during the end-of-day phone calls we exchanged. I'd never had a real boyfriend before, so I was learning all the relevant feelings at the age of twenty-eight. Confusion, lust, pining, and more puzzlement, I ran the full gamut of emotions, and whenever he phoned, I wavered between lust, and what I could only imagine was a powerful affection. I couldn't call it love yet, because love meant long-term, and he was yet to see me at my clumsiest or watch me make a fool of myself, or hell, be unable to choose from a menu if he even got me out of the house to face the terrors of a restaurant. McDonald's wasn't a real date venue, and the drive-through was about my limit anyway.

When he arrived late on a Monday, tired, and smelling faintly of smoke, I hugged him hard, and it turned to kissing, but he was quiet with exhaustion, so we made hot chocolate and sat out on the patio looking at the stars. I felt as if this was normal, and everything in me was calm and centered, although it didn't help that we sat close, and I could feel the warmth of his arm where we touched.

"You know we've never really talked about the DCD," he began, out of the blue, "is there anything I should know? Things that I can do to help."

Yeah, that was *exactly* what I needed, my big bad boyfriend *helping* me, so much for equality in a relationship. "I don't need help," I said.

He reared back. "Shit, I didn't mean it to come out like that, fuck, I'm sorry." He reached for my hand.

I shook him off. "It's okay. I get it." I said.

"No, I meant, hell..." he rubbed at his eyes, "I don't know what I meant. I want to know how you are, and how I can..." he was going to say help, and I was frustrated. "You help me," he blurted, and when he reached for my hand this time I was too surprised to pull back.

"Huh?"

"On bad days, I will sit in the backyard, with Sean and Leo, you know, it might be one of them sometimes, and their days may have been just as bad, but we don't talk about what happened. We give each other space just to be, and when I'm with you, I feel your compassion and your silent acceptance of me just being me, just like I do with my best friends." He leaned close with an earnest expression. "Does that make sense?"

"I guess—"

"So if I can do something back, to be the person you need me to be—"

I cut off his words with a kiss. "You're everything I need you to be right now," I said, firmly. The fact that Eric wanted me was a more significant thing than he would ever know. It was enormous, vital, eternal, but there was no way I was going to tell him that, so I changed direction.

"DCD is a weird thing," I used the word I despised in a very different way than others who'd thrown it at me. "Mom never wavered in her love for me, and I was always just her son whatever I did. I guess though that Dad always found me a confusing mess of contradictions because he'd wanted a ballplayer for a son, and what he'd got was someone very different. I know it must have rocked his world order, but he had my back and deferred to Mom in most things."

"He sounds like a good dad."

"He was. He loved my mom, Nicole, and me, and that made it easier for me to grow up, expecting that they would always support me." I coughed to clear my choked throat. "At the age of ten with the bullying at school and the eternal fears that kept me from finding and keeping friends, I had it pretty freaking bad. Add in dyslexia, and even that one thing every human takes for granted, the ability to record our thoughts, is lost. I can write, I understand language and could fake discussing important things if I needed to, but the day-to-day minutiae of communication escaped me."

I sipped my drink and thought about how to explain everything so far without too many details.

"Mom and Dad were told they couldn't have children, but at forty-one, Mom had Nicole and then three years later, me. If someone told my mom that they'd broken a leg, she would look on the bright side, and with all seriousness inform them that at least the other leg worked. So, faced with a child and the shiny new label she selected carefully from the various parts of DCD like she was choosing from a menu, to conclude that I wasn't as *bad* as I could be. Up until the day we lost her to cancer, she was so outwardly positive that everything would be okay."

"You were perfect to her."

I huffed a laugh as I ran that statement through my mind. "I was an imperfect mess."

"We agreed to disagree," he pulled my hand to kiss the back of it. My heart melted, and it was on the tip of my tongue to tell him I was falling for him.

"So what was it like growing up?"

"Good and bad days. Like Mom said, some kids with my diagnosis had all bad days. I didn't understand math, or reading, or writing, but I had a gift for art. Art was the only thing I could concentrate on for long periods, and for some reason, I could hold a paintbrush or a coloring pencil without even thinking about it. I'm sure there is a fancy name for this, but I know that when I'm drawing, I'm not thinking about failing or the mechanics of what I'm doing."

"Your art is beautiful."

I couldn't help smiling at that. "I want to draw you one

day," I waited for him to bluster and tell me to get lost. Instead, he dropped his hold of my hand and lifted his T-shirt, leaning back on the chair.

"Like one of your French girls?" he asked and ran his tongue over his lips before pouting. I think he expected me to laugh. I know for sure he didn't expect me launching myself at his lap.

And neither of us expected to break the chair.

Although maybe we should have.

SEVENTEEN

Eric

TODAY I FINISHED TOO late to head to Brady's and at first I was pissed at that. But now, chilled was too little of a word to use to describe me. Sprawled on the large sectional, in shorts, bare-chested, with nothing to do but sit and think, I was so relaxed I was nearly asleep.

Add in *Mountain Men* on TV, where Eustace had left the handbrake off his truck and was chasing it down a hill, and I was in heaven. My eyelids were heavy, and I paused the show because I needed to know how Eustace was going to get out of this situation. Settling back, I closed my eyes and thought about the day.

It didn't last long. I was sleeping before I even knew it was coming and only woke when a wet dog landed on my chest, with a Frisbee in his mouth. I jumped sideways, Cap dropped the Frisbee with added pool water, and then plunked his butt on my hand. I heard Leo laughing in the doorway, balled up the T-shirt I'd taken off which was now soaked, and threw it in his direction.

"Lame throw dude," Leo snorted, and then came into

the room and sank back in the opposite seat. He was still in uniform, cradling a mug of coffee and looking tired. I could've made Cap jump on him as well, but yeah, I always respect the blue. "So..." he began, which never boded well.

"What do you want?" I was suspicious.

He raised a single eyebrow as if he was shocked at my reaction, but he forgot I'd known him since he was a kid. Whatever he wanted to say to me would end up with me doing something stupid. Or wrong. Or worse, involved a family get together at Mama Byrne's house.

"Mama is holding a huge barbecue welcome home party for Lorna—"

I knew it. "No, I'm not going to a party for your sister, who's only been away for a month."

"You didn't let me finish."

"Because I know what you're going to say, Mama Byrne has invited a friend to the event, someone she wants me to meet, and you said you'd bring me to whatever she's planning."

"I wouldn't do that," he lied while trying to look innocent, as if butter wouldn't melt.

It was my turn to lift an eyebrow, and he tried his hardest to stay in the moment, then collapsed like a soufflé.

"Okay, she made me promise to bring you, but only because my cousin is in from Seattle and she wants to meet you."

Sometimes being bi was more of a hindrance than a help. She'd put a lot of guys in my way, but the minute

Leo's mom found out I liked women as well, then her pool of potential partners for me had doubled overnight.

"I don't know why she is so fixated on me. She has her sons to take care of first, not to mention three daughters, only one of whom is married."

"Just say you'll come, then she won't corner me."

A fierce Italian woman, Mama Byrne had married a New York cop and ruled her brood with a rod of iron. She was also adorable, soft, warm-hearted and responsible for creating a family with six children who were all adopted. I loved her dearly, always had, and Leo knew I'd agree to go eventually, but that didn't mean I couldn't ride his ass until I did.

"I'll think about it," I said, and scratched Cap under the chin as he rolled onto his back in his sleep. He never woke up once, just calm and happy to be with his humans.

"Then it's a yes."

I closed my eyes and slid back down on the couch. "You owe me," I muttered.

"You're an asshole. I can't wait for Sean to come home."

"He lives next door."

"I might move with him," Leo snarked. "At least he doesn't complain about attending Mama's events."

"Because *she* doesn't try to hook him up the minute he arrives."

We sat in silence for a while, and I waited for the next question, and I knew there would be one because Leo never sat still for long, and he was still on the other couch. I could hear him tapping the side of his mug. Finally, after

I was just about to give up and close my eyes, he went straight for the jugular.

"How is it going with Brady?"

"It's going."

"And?"

"And nothing."

"So he didn't want to see you, and nothing is happening?"

I could've thrown a line in that implied we'd gotten into a routine of sex at every possible moment. I could've even described the fact that the sexual connection we had was off the charts, but I wouldn't. This was private and what the two of us had was different from anything I'd ever experienced before—I just knew it. I didn't want to plan, but he was a funny guy, with his stories about his kids, and the way he expressed himself with his hands, sketching scenes in the air as he spoke. I could fall for him, and I wonder if maybe I was already captivated.

"We see each other," I finally offered, and Leo snorted a laugh.

"You are so gone I see stars in your eyes."

"Fuck you, Five-Oh," I said without heat and settled back on the couch.

"Bring him to the barbecue. Oh, and don't go to sleep, Mia is nearly home."

That was Leo and me. Never mind that our best friend Sean was on his way back, or that he and Ash were all loved up and married. We just wanted our Mia time, and if I wasn't careful, Leo could get her sweet hugs first. I narrowed my eyes at him, and he shrugged as if he wasn't thinking the same thing.

It's on.

"It's my turn."

How many times had I said that in the last hour? Sean and Ash had finally gotten home, and Leo had monopolized Mia way too long. Damn him for making it to the front door first, but sleep had pulled me under and refused to let me go for way too long.

"She prefers her Uncle Leo," Leo stated, and danced around the kitchen a little, Mia in his arms babbling at him. I caught him on the next pass and blocked his way with my best menacing look, and with a pout, he handed Mia to me. "Asshole," he mouthed at me and then watched with narrowed eyes. I turned my back to him and stalked out to the living room where I'd just left Sean and Ash.

"Let's get you away from Uncle Five-Oh," I said and swung her around before settling on the couch. "How are you, Mia?" I asked, and bounced her on my knee, making faces and waiting for her smile.

"Bah, bah," she informed me with a toothy grin and patted my face.

"Why are you telling her my name is Five-Oh?" Leo asked me from the kitchen, where he was now consigned to making coffee, but I ignored him.

"You're right, Mia, Uncle Five-Oh is a baby-hogging-Muppet," I singsonged, hearing Leo's muffled curse.

Sean cleared his throat, and I glanced over at him.

"Muppet is not a bad word," I pointed out, and there was no argument for that. I smooched her face, and she laughed and gripped my hair, and my heart expanded with love for the little tyke, even if she tugged way too hard.

Leo deposited the second round of coffees on the table and stepped back. "So tell us about the honeymoon."

Ash was curled into Sean's side, both of them tucked as much as two grown men could be into the corner of the facing couch. I'd seen them like this before, always touching, never far apart, and familiar envy spiked in me. I'd never experienced real love but was sure that one day it would happen accidentally, as it had for Sean, but that didn't mean I didn't appreciate the love that Ash and Sean shared.

Mia fell asleep on my chest, just as Ash was explaining how he and Sean had taken Mia for a swim and how excellent she was. I didn't have to say anything at all. Of course, Mia was excellent—she was the absolute best at everything.

I had two day-shifts followed by two night-shifts before going into having four days off, which was eaten into by volunteering with other firefighters beating the remnants of the Harvey fire. Every second of my work was focused, and things only changed when I was back home, and my first thought was always something to do with Brady. What was he doing? Was he okay? Did he want to see me? I'd kept going with my research into DCD and I think I was getting a sense of the way his brain worked to analyze the world around him.

I had this insane idea that I would ask him to come

with me to Mama Byrne's thing, and not just because that would get everyone off my back. I wanted them to meet him. I wanted him to talk to Sean and Ash, and meet Mia properly, and help me prank Leo. Only I had a strong sense that what we had was fragile and I'd found out that some people with DCD weren't good in crowds or chaos, and eating with the Byrne clan was both of those things and more.

But, it was like that whole issue of a tree falling in the woods and whether it makes a sound. If I didn't share Brady with people was what we had even real?

"Are you ill?" Leo poked my belly.

"Huh?" I grabbed at his hand, but he was way too quick for me and put the counter between us before I could react.

"You look constipated," he summarized as he poured fresh coffee into a to-go cup.

"It's because I live with you," was my catchall answer.

"Ha, freaking ha," Leo snarked. "But seriously dude, when you think all deep, and your face is all mushed up, it's only right I ask if you've had a shit this morning."

I threw a dishrag at him, but it missed and landed on the chair behind.

"Go to work, Five-oh."

He checked the lid on his cup, then left with a final wink. I gave him the finger just so he was aware of how I felt about his asshattery.

Today was the first real time I had gotten an entire morning to myself, and sue me if I showered at the speed of sound, then set off early so that I could be at Brady's place the very moment Maddie and Lucas had left for school. After much thinking and worrying and contemplating all the possible outcomes, I'd already decided how this morning would go. When I got to his house, I wouldn't kiss him, or go to my knees, or carry him somewhere so we could get off. Today we would spend some time talking like I would on a regular date, and I wouldn't lose control and show him how much I wanted him.

But then, Brady opened the door.

EIGHTEEN

Brady

As soon as Eric was inside, I threw myself at him. Or he scooped me up. I don't know who moved first and I didn't care, because this time we headed for the stairs and *this time* there would be a bed involved. I was already close to losing my shit by the time he tossed me onto the bed. It had taken three tries for him to get us into the right bedroom, and finally, we'd managed it, but not before spending way too long rutting and shoving and kissing against every available surface. He was everything I wanted, and I needed it *now*.

"Lube? Condoms?"

I sprawled on the bed and gestured at my drawer, thanking the heavens I'd thought to stock up.

"We need to talk," Eric announced as he stripped with efficiency, which was hella sexy, then passed me the condom before snapping the top of the lube. It didn't seem to me that he wanted to talk at all, unless *talk* was another word for fucking me.

I held the condom out to him, but he shook his head.

"Talk about what?" I asked.

"Will you…?" He gestured at himself and looked shy.

"You want me to…" I was just as shy. How fucking stupid was this?

"Uh-huh."

I was clumsy with the condom, frustrated, not so much with my innate awkwardness, but because Eric wanted me to fuck him. *Make love to him.*

He took over, kissing, and sucking, and we writhed together, and the power I had over this man was incredible. He was going to move onto all fours, but I wanted what we'd had before, I wanted to stare into his eyes.

When I was inside, when I had him whimpering and pleading, I was a god, and every molecule of me was on the edge. I don't know how I lasted. I wasn't sure how long we'd been going. I didn't care, but when he took himself in hand, and I reared back to watch him come, he had his eyes open, and he cursed. I followed not long after, holding so still that I could hear my ragged breathing, and when I climbed off, flopping to the mattress, spent, the chill of the AC pebbled my sensitive nipples and cooled my skin.

"Holy shit," Eric murmured, and then flailed an arm until he could catch my hand, which he gripped and held on to. "That was so fucking hot."

"God yeah," I managed, and laced my fingers with his. I'd made it to twenty-eight without much more than hookups, and even then they'd been few and far between. It was difficult to meet guys for sex when I deliberately decided to stay in or near the damn house. Spencer filled some of the spaces, but that was my only outside male contact for now, and I wasn't yanking him inside. Not to mention he was straight, and married, with two children, so yeah, not happening.

I wondered if it was even possible to have this intense incendiary sex with anyone else. Had I just been missing out? Maybe it was out there more than I'd thought. Or was it just us, and that our chemistry was explosive?

We lay in silence, and when my breathing settled, I let out a low whistle. DCD was insidious and part of every second of my life, but just then, when I was pushing into Eric and making him lose his freaking mind, I was powerfully invincible. DCD could go fuck itself because I'd won that battle.

"Tell me about the children."

I extricated my hand from his vise-like grip and turned on my side to face him, gaze skimming from his broad chest to his thick thighs and back up again, stopping for a while to focus on the hair that thickened up to his chest. I buried my fingers in there and tugged, then smoothed my hand down to his stomach, which had fast become my favorite part of him. He was cut, physically beautiful, but his belly was a little softer, and I rested my cheek there for a moment as he threaded his fingers through my hair.

"What do you want to know?" I didn't know why I'd even asked that. It was obvious he would want to know the circumstances around me being uncle/dad to my niece and nephew. At least this was us talking, even if I had gone straight to sex as soon as I saw him instead of what I'd planned, which had been us sitting and having a civilized conversation.

There had been nothing civilized about that sex, and I

winced at the clear bite mark on his shoulder. At least I hadn't marked him where he couldn't hide it, although what if he was getting changed at the firehouse?

"Tell me you don't all shower naked together," I blurted.

"What?"

"With all the other firefighters, together, naked."

He did that eyebrow raise he had down to a tee. "Is that a fantasy of yours?" He chuckled.

"No. Yes. No." Fuck, I could feel myself going scarlet. I pointed at his shoulder, "I gave you a bruise."

He tried to look down at the crazy angle but wouldn't have been able to see it without a mirror, then shrugged. "No worries, that's also kind of hot, and no, we have separate showers," he lowered his voice. "Are you disappointed?" He rolled up to kiss me, and I could see where this was going, straight past talking and right onto more sex.

That's a great idea, my cock suggested.

Do you even want to get to know the man, my brain asked.

Sex is good, cock added.

I supposed it was, and I guessed this thing with Eric was not a grand love affair where we needed to talk, brain agreed.

See, you should listen to me more often. Was I the only person who had an inner-cock who always got his own way?

I closed my eyes briefly to focus my thoughts, which was difficult considering my cock was winning the battle. I should've avoided discussions of fantasy and instead focused solely on the question he'd asked me. It seemed as if he had the same idea, shuffling out of my reach and propping his head on his hands. He took up so much of the bed, sprawled there, sexy, and I wanted him again. Already.

Get your head straight, dude. Was that my brain or my cock? Was there any difference between the two?

"So tell me everything," Eric prompted me and poked my hand to pull me back to the here and now.

"Huh?" I'd lost track of where we were in the conversation.

"You asked me what I wanted to know about how you came to have the children."

"Oh. Yeah. I was babysitting. Dan had come home on leave after he was injured by an IED and was recuperating, nearly ready to go back. That was the entire focus in the house, how dangerous it was being deployed. It was their wedding anniversary, and Nicole, my sister, was so content to have him home. When she asked me to babysit for Lucas and Maddie I was happy to do it, I mean I was in this house more than I was in my crappy rented apartment back home anyway, so it was a pleasure to spend time with the kids. But then it all went wrong." My breath hitched, the emotion tight in my throat.

"You don't have to," Eric murmured. "I'm sorry I asked."

"No, it's okay, I guess it's the next thing isn't it."

"The next thing?"

"Lust, then sex, then a shitload of background information."

He frowned at me, although it was more of a fleeting

concern than an expression that stayed. Maybe I'd misworded myself, or he didn't agree with that extra bit about information. Who knew? It wasn't as though I could read his micro-expressions.

I pressed on, "Lucas was four, Maddie two. A drunk driver who swerved into their lane, my sister died immediately. First responders managed to cut Dan from the car, and there was still hope for him, but a few days later he was gone. I was here that night with Lucas and Maddie, and I just never left."

"I'm sorry," Eric sighed. "I've seen accidents, drinking, idiots running red lights, and it's horrific for the families left behind. Even when a person is wracked with grief if they can carry on for others, then that is brave. You stepped up for your sister, and I admire you for that."

Brave? I didn't feel courageous.

"Nicole and Dan named me as guardian, and that was who I had to be. When we first lost them I was done—I wasn't a functioning human being, I was in a black place, I'd lost my only real friend, and then I had two children to look out for."

"I'm sorry," he murmured.

"It is what it is," I said in my usual dismissive way. Only it hit me that Eric deserved better than that, hell, I deserved it too. "Actually no, it was shit, but I couldn't let the grief of everything consumes myself. Mom wasn't with us any longer, and Dad passed away maybe two months after we lost Nicole. The doctors had no idea why, just that he had a broken heart." Recalling the weight of everything back then, I shuddered and closed my eyes. "I had moments every single day when I was adamant that Lucas and Maddie had a real family, even though it was just us. Some days I would sit and people-watch at the local store, and check out other parents. I'd play the what-if game. Like, what if that couple over there had a house with a pool, or what if they had more money than I'd inherited and could give Maddie and Lucas everything they needed. What if they were more intelligent than me, not as clumsy as me, what if their genetics weren't as fucked up—"

He rolled on top of me so hard the breath left my chest in a *whoosh*.

"No," he kissed me savagely, only gentling when I wrapped my hands around the back of his neck and held on for the ride. When he pulled back, there was a determination in his gaze. "You stayed."

"Yeah, I stayed for a week, then a month, a year, I saw their birthdays pass, and slowly we became something different."

"You decided to stay and be their dad."

"The decision to be there for them wasn't carefully weighed; it just *was*. I went to court to get probate guardianship. Dan didn't have siblings, and his parents were more interested in themselves than their grandchildren. I was the only one, and there weren't any guarantees, but I went through the process for formal adoption proceedings. The courts don't care about blood relatives, they cared about legal relatives, and Nicole and Dan had made sure everything was in place. It wasn't much of a fight for me to get the adoption passed." I paused. Attempting to sum up that whole journey was hard. Did Eric want or need to know all of this? "At grief counseling, I met Spencer, and he didn't judge me or misunderstand me, and then he and his wife became part of my life as well. It was enough."

"No one gives you a guide on how things are in life," he said, "I bet it wasn't easy."

"There were nights when Lucas cried for his mom, and his dad, and for what had happened to him and his sister, how they'd been left alone with me. He would have temper tantrums, act out, but somehow we got through it. Maddie was different, she was only two, and memories of her mom were shadows that faded quickly. I never took down a single photo," I said immediately, when I realized I sounded as if I was okay with Maddie forgetting her parents. I wasn't okay. *It wasn't okay.*

"Did you have the time to grieve when you lost your sister?"

"Yeah," I lied. Dealing with the grief had come later when it had finally hit me. My beautiful sister was gone.

"You, Maddie, and Lucas are a real family," Eric said, moved off me, and tugged me closer until I was snuggled under his arm, my head on his chest.

I could've said that I agreed we were a real family. But instinct always made me play down what I would do for the children, I could make it sound as if I didn't care at all, but none of that was true. I might not have been the best dad for them, but I was the best goddamn uncle I could be. "Yeah. A real one."

We lay in silence for a while, and then Eric cleared his throat.

"So you can say no, and I totally understand, but Leo's mama is holding this barbecue thing, lots of kids that Maddie and Lucas would have met at the wedding, but there will be quiet corners as well, I promise you. I want to show you off, and I promise I won't leave your side."

No. God no. It's too fast. I can't do this. What is happening, fuck, I'm a mess.

He wants to show me off? The kids would have fun? He won't leave me alone.

He makes me feel safe.

"Okay," I agreed.

What the hell have I just done?

NINETEEN

Eric

WHEN BRADY OPENED THE DOOR, he looked ready to visit at the barbecue. In cut-offs, a smart shirt, and with his hair styled, he was perfect, and what I wanted to do was pull him close and kiss him hello. However, the expression on his face was a warning, and I knew how to read it. He was getting ready to slam the door in my face, even though Lucas and Maddie were behind him, each carrying covered dishes.

"We made salads," Maddie explained and weaved her way past Brady to join me outside. Lucas followed close after, and we exchanged a quick fist bump as he balanced whatever dish he had in one hand.

"Truck's open, we'll be out in a minute," I said, and stepped into the house, easing Brady's hand from the door and pulling it shut behind me. "Hey," I held onto him and guided him to the couch where we did our best thinking. "Talk to me."

"I went to a parent-teacher conference when Maddie

was seven," he began, then shook my hand free. "You won't believe what I did there, but I can't go back."

"Did you fall over?" I went right for lightening the tone, but he was so serious I doubted I'd be able to get him out of it.

"It was worse than that. The teacher, who was incredibly proud of Maddie, showed me some writing, and I was proud as well, that my beautiful niece was so clever in her class. Only, I couldn't read it, the letters blurred, danced," he moved his hands as if he was sketching the words, and my heart broke for him. "No one laughed at me, no one even knew, but it didn't matter, because what if people did know?"

"You shouldn't worry that they'd look at Maddie and Lucas differently. Wait until you meet Leo's mama, and then you'll see what he had to put up with at school. One day he got into a fight, y'know, I don't know what about, but Mama Byrne was up that school giving everyone a piece of her mind. I think the other students admired Leo for having someone who would stand up for him." I smiled at Brady, thinking that I'd scored a win with that one.

"You don't understand, I worry every day that Maddie and Lucas will have trouble because I'm the weird dad who doesn't go to the school, or drive, that they might be bullied, I mean it's a real worry, okay?"

"I understand—"

"But it isn't only that. What if the school judged me and thought I wasn't the right person for Maddie and Lucas?"

The realization hit me like a sledgehammer. This wasn't about people laughing at Brady, or teasing the kids, or bullying at school. This was about losing the children altogether?!

"But, you told me you adopted them, right?"

"I did."

"So legally, they are your children, you're their dad, and the judge must have seen something in you to grant you adoption rights." I was confused that he would think anything else.

"See this is it," he was miserable. "I know I'm a good dad, I'm an accomplished artist, I keep up with cooking, and finances, and vacation plans, and then it takes one shitty thought, and I spiral, and then we end up here." He huffed loudly.

I sat back on the couch and considered the best way to approach this.

"There's been too many times when men have wanted me because I fit their idea of the hero firefighter they want in their bed. I want to talk to them, watch movies, have them get pushy in bed, help me be my best self. There would be days when I'll need you to be there for me, when I see something that hurts me, or when I fail, and I know you will be there, understanding me, and loving me right back. We can talk about the garden, and the kids, and art, and we'll kiss and hug and make love. You can stop me from spiraling, and I can do the same right back. So tell me what I can do?"

"Let me stay here," he tilted his chin as if he was daring me to say no.

"You want me to leave you, and just take the kids with me?"

"Yes."

"No, that's not going to happen. Together, we'll work out how I can make this better for you, and then we'll figure a way for you to protect me from Mama Byrne and her need to feed me, and then we can find a quiet, isolated corner of her huge sprawling garden, and we can eat and drink, and you can maybe meet a couple of my friends if you want, but you don't have to. Only, I'm so lucky to be with you, and I want everyone to see how blessed I am. Nothing will happen, you will be your amazing sexy self, and you could take your sketchbook, and draw caricatures of people and, if it gets too much we can have a word you use, like apple or frog or something, and I will scoop you up in a fireman lift, and I will carry you out of there like you're a king."

Brady concentrated hard on what I was saying and went from angry to confused to smiling.

"Frog or Apple, got it," he smirked, "And you want me to draw caricatures?"

"And eat extra food that Mama Byrne gives me, and maybe talk to Leo for a bit so he can see who I'm falling in love with." He was startled, and his mouth fell open, and I realized what I'd done, so I repeated the words in case he thought I'd thrown them out in some unfounded grand gesture. "I'm falling in love with you, Brady. I want everyone to meet you. Come with me and see how it goes?"

He nodded, and I took that as a victory, standing and offering a hand that he took. We collected sketchbooks and pens, locked up the house and headed for the truck, the kids bickering in the back over a game on Lucas' phone. Brady buckled up and then half turned to speak to them.

"Lucas, I don't want to see you on your phone all afternoon, please."

Lucas seemed as if he was going to argue, but then he caught my gaze in the mirror and looked back at Brady. I was backing whatever Brady was saying, and maybe I was exactly what I needed to be at that moment. It wasn't my place, but I was passive reinforcement, in a way.

"Okay, Uncle Brady," he made a deliberate show of turning off the phone and putting it into his pocket.

By the time we arrived at Mama Byrne's, the four of us had worked our way through an entire packet of Haribo, and sung along to random songs on the radio. I forgot fire, and worry, and life, and just focused on love, and when we got there, Brady held my hand and Maddie held the other. As if it was an everyday event.

I wanted it to be an everyday event.

Mama Byrne was very much in charge today, and it was apparent from the moment we arrived. She knew exactly what food was where, counted heads as we arrived, and told us where to sit, and seemed to have an instinctive kinship with Brady, not fussing over him too much and certainly lowering her voice from its usual full volume. She hugged me though, and let out a stream of rapid Italian, none of which I could ever hope to understand.

"Mama, leave Eric alone," Leo appeared at our side, and in a smooth move, he whisked us away from her with a few words in Italian of his own. She laughed at whatever he said.

"What did you say to her?"

"That her Eric has someone at his side and that cousin Maria has lost out."

I introduced Leo to Brady, Maddie, and Lucas, and the children left to deliver salads and headed right for the group of kids hanging around a big trampoline. Leo and Brady shook hands, and Leo was his most charming self, mostly at my expense.

"Did he tell you about the cherry yogurt incident?" Leo asked, and I smacked him on the back, making him spill his beer.

"What about cherry yogurt?" Brady asked with a sparkling light in his eyes.

I clapped a hand over Leo's mouth, and we wrestled for a moment before Leo backed off and held up his hands. "Okay, okay, I won't tell him, but can I tell him about the skunk?"

"We're leaving," I announced, and guided Brady away faster than he probably expected. Still, he was laughing, and when we found our quiet corner, he couldn't wait to ask.

"So, cherry yogurt, and a skunk, you want to explain that?"

I started and stopped the story about the yogurt a lot of times. People found us in our corner, but Brady smiled and nodded to everyone, and talked sometimes, and other times he concentrated on drawing. I think the images he concentrated on creating were a barrier to the people around us. He had his sketchbook on his knees and drew small caricatures that captured likenesses perfectly. Word must have gotten around because I never did get to tell him the story about the skunk. I thought that could wait for another day.

Maddie and Lucas checked in on us every so often;

they'd made friends with Frankie's kids and didn't want to stay around the oldies, as Lucas put it. They'd set up a slip and slide, and miracle of miracles, Lucas asked Brady to watch over his phone—Brady was as surprised as I was.

"You know I never asked you about your family," he said after they'd left.

I paused a moment to get my thoughts in order, wondering how much he could hear right now without freaking out. My dad had a job that made him public property, and I wanted to take this a step at a time. It wasn't as if I went around using my full double-barreled surname so he wouldn't put two and two together until I was honest with him. But none of it seemed right, and what the hell was I not telling him for? I imagined a week or two down the road when Leo or Sean said something by accident.

"I'm an only child. Mom is a homemaker. Dad might be something that means... *um*... look there's no easy way to say this, but he's a US Senator."

He looked at me sharply. "Huh?"

"It's a private thing for me. I don't even use my full name and—"

"What is your actual name then?" He didn't sound pissed, just interested.

"Eric Lester-Hythe."

"You're Senator Lester-Hythe's son."

"That's what it says on my birth certificate." I smiled and waited for him to run for the hills, but he sat there silently and watched me until I wriggled in my chair. "Tell me that's okay. I mean, the spotlight isn't on me, or you, and when I see Mom it's effortless and relaxed, and Dad is always working, so I see him maybe four times a year plus Christmas." I was rambling, and I needed to stop.

"What did they think about their son being...?" he waved a pencil.

"A firefighter or being gay?"

"Both, either, I guess."

"They took both things in stride. The real issue was me skipping college to become a firefighter. We're close in our own way, they're good parents, just not in the same way as Leo and his family are."

"Do you see a lot of them?"

"On rare occasions, I get trotted out for events as the resident hero son, which gets them brownie points, but mostly I hide away here and live my own life. I see them for all the big occasions and some of the little ones. I'll introduce you one day." He went quiet, but I had expected that—the thought of meeting my parents, particularly ones in the public eye, would terrify even the most confident of men. "Not for a long time though," I reassured, and he nodded, before going back to his drawing.

As I watched him sketch, focused, and smiling to himself, I realized something fundamental, and it wasn't until nearly everyone had left and it had grown dark that I felt I could tell him.

"Brady?"

"Hmm?" He looked up from the bag where he was stowing his art supplies and smiled at me as I leaned over and kissed him.

"I'm not just falling in love with you," I said. "I know it's quick, I get you might not believe me, but I can't imagine life without you. It could be because of what I do, and the things I see, but I think about you all the time, Brady. You're my happy place, and I know for sure that I love you, and that I want more. Like a lifetime of more."

He shuffled back, and I wished there was more light so I could get a read on his expression.

"You know that I can't process things as fast as you," he stood, and the chair fell back. I stood immediately in case he needed me. He didn't; he was hoisting his bag on his shoulder and seemed determined. "But thank you for what you said."

"Is it okay if I say it again?"

He looked uncertain for a moment and then he smiled. "Yeah."

I told him I loved him when we got home. I told him as he made hot chocolate, I told him again when we were making love, and then when I kissed him goodbye as I headed to the station.

He cradled my face at that last kiss, met my gaze, and smiled.

"Give me time to sort through the mess in my thoughts?"

I hugged him, and I had to have the last word.

"Of course."

TWENTY

Brady

I SPENT much of the next week in a daze. He loved me, and I'd been so close to saying I loved him too. I must have operated as usual, on some level—the kids were in school each day, with lunches, and I recall talking to them about homework and how I was sure that Eric would go to the next career day if Lucas asked him. Not to mention the other things like signing forms, handing out money, and being able to help Maddie with her art homework.

Somehow, that small win was enough to carry me to the weekend, but I needed to get the rest of Friday over first. Eric called when he could, but he'd worked four days again this week, with only a few eight-hour breaks in between. I knew it was supposed to be twenty-four hours on and then twenty-four off to rest, but somehow that wasn't happening right now, and I couldn't help worrying. So with the dazed love thing, and the worrying, and the kids, I didn't do much in the way of work.

What I did have was a fully worked out storyboard for a children's book. It had started on Monday when the kids had left for school. I'd tried my hardest to focus when they first left, but found myself doodling teddies dressed in firefighter helmets trying to put out a fire in a house owned by a scarecrow called Sid. I'd even named the two teddy heroes Fluff and Ted, and I didn't think it was a long shot to say that Ted was based on Eric, particularly when I began to shade the fur around his ears with gray. Then there was the talking engine because every kids' story needed an inanimate object that talked, it was shiny and perfect, and I'd asked Eric to show me pictures of his engine online. When he'd asked why and I'd lied that it was something I was doing in my spare time, he sent me photos. When I found myself staring out of the window thinking about a name for the talking truck I knew it was time to go out for a walk, or tidy the house, or go into the garden, anything that would break the lack of concentration on what I should be doing.

As I passed the door, the bell rang, and a surge of excitement hit me. Eric was here. Somehow, he'd not had to work today, despite the news I'd seen about a new fire sixty miles from here, and he was at my door. I flung the door open in my haste to see him, getting a face full of wood as it slammed back on me, and I ended up on my ass on the floor.

"Shit, Brady, are you okay?"

Spencer loomed over me, and not just him, but Ben the post guy as well. They both stared at me, and there was a horrifically silent exchange of reactions. This could've gone one of two ways. I could ignore it had happened, shut the door on them both, and go about my day. Or I could be honest for once.

"Fuck," I cursed, and took Spencer's hand to stand, "No, I'm not all right." I was disoriented, and he guided me to the couch and sat me down, Ben trailing us.

How I love having an audience.

I forced that sarcastic self-pity back down where it was rising from, and instead, I smirked at them both.

"Talk about dramatic," I deadpanned.

Spencer raised an eyebrow and looked as if he was about to ask me what the hell was going on.

"Do you need me to call 911?" Ben asked.

"God, no," I said immediately. I shook my arms and wriggled a little in an effort to show him I was okay.

"Cool, so, this is for you," he held out a parcel and backed away, then with a cheery wave he left.

"More paints?" Spencer asked as he walked into the kitchen.

"I didn't order any."

At least I didn't think I'd put an order in. Maybe I'd been carried away by the scarlet of the fire engine and ordered twelve different reds. If I did, then I'd completely forgotten it. I shook the parcel, but it wasn't heavy as if it had tubes of paint in it, and I couldn't think of anything else I'd order. Then I saw the CALFIRE label on the back, and excitement curled in my chest. Had Eric sent me something? How had he found the time to do that?

I picked at the tape and opened the small box, lifting out a soft toy, a lion in a yellow uniform with a red firefighter's helmet and a tiny ax. There was a card in there as well, and I put the toy to one side to read it. Spencer knew enough not to help me with understanding the information, but right now, I was eager to make sense of the dancing letters that I couldn't distinguish. It was a handwritten card, and that made it even harder to read. I understood a few words, but yeah, speed was of the essence here, so I handed it to Spencer.

"You sure?" he asked, and I nodded as I picked up the soft toy again.

Spencer cleared his throat. "Hi Brady, I work in the office where Eric is stationed. He asked that I send you this cuddly toy and to tell you that this is a mountain lion called Cal, but that he prefers the idea of a teddy bear. Best, Adam." Spencer paused and then passed the card to me. I put it back in the box but kept the lion in a tight hold, then emotions flooding me were overwhelming, and I didn't know what to do with them. A great affection, and desire, confusion, worry, but feeling lucky, and most of all, loved.

"I've been watching the news," I blurted, because right in the dark center of me it was fear that knotted there. "About the fires." I looked up at Spencer, who regarded me as if he expected me to cry or shout or do something super weird. "I wish I'd told him I'd fallen all the way, that it wasn't just me wanting to be with him, and near him, that I love him completely. What if he doesn't come home, what if…"

Spencer sat next to me and put an arm over my shoulders, but he didn't give me any wise counsel, there was no advice about how I could tell him when I saw him. We just sat for the longest time in complete silence.

"As your best friend, I want to meet this Eric, because I have to tell him that if he hurts you, I'll hurt him, you know that, right?" He had laughter in his tone, and when he squeezed my shoulder, I leaned into his support, and I grinned so hard that I thought my face might crack.

Friday night dinner at the house was always taco night, and it involved me, Lucas, and Maddie making things up as we went along. Even after a hard week, it was the one time when all the rules went out the window, and each of us could have whatever we wanted in our tacos. During the week there would be outlandish ideas—case in point Maddie announcing she wanted nothing but corn in hers this week, but by the Friday the ingredients fell into the bacon and the roasted vegetable categories.

"So Jemima's mom said I could have a sleepover after the party," Maddie began, and I winced inside. Jemima's party was *the* social engagement of Maddie's school year, and there was going to be magic, and face painting, both of which had Maddie visibly vibrating with excitement when she'd showed me the invite.

"That should be okay if I can talk to Jemima's mom." I just needed to do my checks as any responsible uncle would do. "Can you ask her to call me?"

"Okay, and can I take my pink sleeping bag and my Sparkles pony set?"

"The sleeping bag yes, but if anything happens to Sparkles pony, you'll be very sad."

She put another pile of tomato in her mixing bowl, not so much cut as squeezed into pieces. "I won't."

I started to reply, but Lucas beat me to it, and I should have known how it would go since he'd come home from school in a mutinously lousy mood. "Remember you cried when you left Sparkles at the store? You cried so hard you were sick." He was joking with his sister, but there was an anger in his voice that I hadn't heard before. "Anyway Jemima is stupid, face painting is for babies, and—"

"That's enough," I interrupted.

He stared at me, then dropped his knife to the counter. "I'm not hungry anyway," he did a complete one-eighty, heading upstairs. The slam of the door was enough to tell me that whatever had put him in a bad mood wasn't lifting now he was home. I wasn't going to chase after him. That was wasn't how things were done in this house, because confrontations messed with my thoughts and I learned a long time ago that thinking space is far better than me storming upstairs demanding to know what was going on.

Maddie sighed and then peered around me up to the stairs. "Lucas cried today, more than I did when I lost Sparkles," she said in a low voice, and went back to her tomato chopping. She was concentrating so hard that the tip of her tongue poked out, but I had to interrupt her.

"Do you know why he was crying?" I asked in a similarly soft voice.

"He wouldn't tell me," she said, with a sniff. "Do you think it's because he didn't get an invite to Jemima's party?"

I smiled inside but answered her in all seriousness. "I don't think so, sweetheart."

We chopped in silence some more, and then she sighed. "Jemima has a second dad, you know. She doesn't call him Uncle or anything."

I knew Jemima's mom, Harriet or something, had

remarried after her first husband passed away. I vaguely remembered the husband from the times he'd dropped Maddie at home after playdates.

"Okay," I said, because she was staring at me for an answer.

"She calls him Dad because he helps her mom out and makes Jemima her lunches and took her to Disney and loves her an awful lot."

"That's lovely," I added onion to my bowl then began to break the bacon into tiny pieces.

"So I know you're not Dad Two, 'cause we can't have those, but can I call you Dad instead, the same as Jemima does?"

I didn't even think to say a word. Instead, I scooped her into a hug, onion hands included, and held her tight, kissing her head.

"I would love that," I said.

"He's not our dad!" Lucas shouted from the top of the stairs, thundering down them and coming to a sliding stop three feet from me and Maddie hugging. His hands were bunched in fists at his side, and he was scarlet. "You're not our dad."

Maddie, bless her, moved between us, "He is so." She defended, but I couldn't have her in the way of her brother, who was seriously in need of me staying calm and thoughtful.

"Let's talk about this, Lucas—"

"No, you're not our dad, you're useless and broken up, and I hate you!"

Maddie flew at Lucas, shouting back at him, and Lucas tried to fend off her punches, tears streaming down his face. The chaos was overwhelming, and I couldn't make sense of it all, humiliation and fear crashing through me. I needed to do something, call Spencer, stop this happening.

I stepped away from the counter, the uproar of two children shouting and the tears, all too much for me.

You're the strongest man I've ever met.

Eric's words snapped into my head. All I needed to do was focus. I could handle this, stay calm, be able to help. I managed to separate Maddie and Lucas, and after a few words of encouragement, I got Maddie to sit on the couch and watch cartoons while I talked to Lucas. He stood there staring at me, crying quietly as if he couldn't stop. He was whispering something on repeat, and I moved closer.

"I'm sorry, please don't go. I'm sorry, please don't go."

I gathered him into my arms and held him as he sobbed against my shirt. I was at a loss of how to deal with this, but somehow, I made it to the bottom step of the stairs, and we sat down.

"I'm not going anywhere, Lucas, I promise."

"You don't *have* to stay, you're not our dad," his voice wavered, and there were more tears.

I hugged him into my side. "You're my children, and I will love you forever, never leave you. I adopted you, Lucas, you know that. So you want to tell me what this is really about? I heard you were crying at school, what's wrong?"

He looked up at me, fear in his eyes. "The school called you? Am I in trouble?"

"No, but you're worrying me here. Can you tell me what's happening?"

"If I tell you," he stopped and wiped his face on his

sleeve, "Will you promise not to go and leave Maddie? I can leave, I'll go and live somewhere else."

What the hell was going on that my twelve-year-old child was telling me he'd leave home?

"Talk to me, Lucas—"

"Promise!"

"I promise." I held up my pinkie, and we swore on it just as usual.

"I hit Cam. I hit him so hard that his nose started to bleed, and he said he was going to get me arrested."

Cam? His best friend, Cameron?

"That's wrong, Lucas, to hit people, you know that." There, I'd done the dad bit. Now I softened my tone. "Tell me why."

"I can't."

"Yes, you can. Tell me quickly, like pulling off a Band-Aid."

Lucas let out a shaky breath and then nodded. "Cam said he wanted money and that he'd hurt Maddie, and you can't come in and help me stop him, so I took your money and gave it to him, but I didn't have any today so he said he'd push Maddie over and hurt her. So I punched him."

I attempted to unpick the sentence, alternating between shame that he felt he couldn't talk to me, or that I couldn't help, alongside fury that a kid was bullying Lucas and extorting him for money.

"You should have told me."

"I didn't want to upset you."

I forced aside any rising self-pity and focused on Lucas. "I will always be there for you."

"But if the teachers want to talk to you, then you'd

have to go into the school. They won't come to the house to see you."

Fuck. Determination gave me a jolt; adrenalin gave me confidence. I could do this. I could go to school because I had to. I was strong, and no one would point and laugh. My children needed me to step up.

"I'll call on Monday, set a meeting, and we'll get this cleared up." I was surprised the school hadn't contacted me, so maybe Cam hadn't gone to the principal, maybe Lucas hadn't hit him as hard as it sounded.

Maddie clambered onto my lap and wrapped her arms around my neck.

"It's okay, Dad, you and Lucas will save me from the nasty boys, I know you will."

My entire world was in my arms, Maddie pressing a kiss to my cheek, Lucas gripping my arm, and something crystalized in that moment as I looked over at the stuffed mountain lion next to the television. I wanted to expand my world to include Eric because he told me I was strong, and a good dad, and he wasn't blowing smoke up my ass. He truly believed it as much as Maddie did.

"You're not stupid," Lucas murmured, "you're the greatest artist in the whole world ever, and you make the best peanut butter and jelly sandwiches."

It seemed like I had Lucas on my side as well.

We were nearly finished with the tacos, the tears were forgotten, but there was a tender new-found connection between the three of us, when the doorbell rang. Yet again I got my hopes up that it was Eric, and yet again I was disappointed until I saw the woman with the red hair and the boy lurking behind her—Cam and his mom, Caroline.

"Hi, Brady, Cam has something to say to you, Lucas, and Maddie."

"I'm sorry," Cam muttered.

"And?" Caroline urged.

Cam tipped his chin in fake confidence. "I'm sorry I've been so mean. It won't happen again." Then he slumped as if he was waiting for the ax to fall.

I exchanged glances with Cam's mom who'd been crying, her eyes puffy, and her pale, freckled skin red.

"Come in, guys," I took a careful step back. "We have ice cream."

"We shouldn't stay," Caroline murmured, but Cam had already stepped in.

"Hey," he said to Lucas and held out a fist. Lucas did the whole fist bump thing back, but it was reluctant, "I'm sorry."

Lucas looked at me then back at Cameron. "I hurt you good," he said.

Cam nodded furiously, "You did, I think you nearly broke my nose, there was blood in lumps. It was super gross."

"How many lumps?" Lucas asked as Maddie made a disgusted face.

"Five at least."

"Cool." They fist-bumped again, this time with feeling.

Just like that, it seemed as if everything was calm in Lucas/Cam world, but that didn't take away the matter of what in holy hell had happened.

"We're going upstairs," Lucas dragged Maddie with him until it was just me and Caroline in the kitchen.

"Ice cream or wine?" I asked, and she gave me a

watery smile before holding out an envelope which I took. Inside was a whole pile of money, maybe a hundred dollars or so in fives and tens, along with a handful of coins.

"That's yours," she said, "he thought we might need it, if... My husband, John lost his job, and his healthcare, and we needed help for my daughter's diabetes, and Cam must have overheard us talking. John is back at work, but he has six months to work before he qualifies for healthcare, Cam wanted to give us the money to help." The words fell out of her in a rush, and she looked mortified by what she was saying.

I opened the freezer drawer and pulled out a tub of Rocky Road, anything not to have to deal with the overwhelming compassion that stole my voice. Scooping out a small mountain into a bowl, I then handed it to her.

"Let's go and sit in the garden." I let her go first, then followed.

We sat in the shade and I listened with compassion and silence, and at the end I realized with all of this, understanding Cameron, forgiving him, loving Lucas and Maddie, being a dad, maybe it was time that I believed in myself because no one was sabotaging my journey to become a better person, I was doing to myself.

Maybe it was up to *me* to be the strong one.

When everything was quiet, kids asleep, Rocky Road gone, and Cameron and his mom home, I was alone in my garden sitting and breathing in the cooling night air.

This was my moment of peace, and when my cell chimed with a text from Eric to say he was at the front door, I couldn't get there fast enough. I bumped into two walls on the way to him, but as soon as I opened it to see him smiling, I tugged Eric inside.

"I love you," I said.

He smelled of citrus, but there was also the hint of smoke, he'd come to me after the fire today, and he needed me as much as I needed him. He looked puzzled at first, and then a smile split his face, "I love you back," he pushed the door shut with his foot.

"When did you finish?"

"Maybe five hours, I don't know, I've lost track of time."

He held me tight, but I felt I was the one holding him upright, and we went to the couch in unison. He slumped down and yawned behind his hand, before blinking at me as if he didn't know exactly where he was.

I put on a movie, I didn't care what it was and moved into the corner of the couch, encouraging him to lean on me. He slid closer and slumped next to me, and in my arms, he slept.

TWENTY-ONE

Eric

"Hello," someone said as I opened my eyes. Maddie was perched on the coffee table and staring at me as if I was an exhibit in a zoo. I raised my arm to look at my watch, but it was all blurry, and I was still so damn tired.

"Hey, Maddie," I replied.

She dimpled a smile. "You remember my name."

"I do."

"Whatcha doing on the couch?" she asked, her legs swinging.

And that was how our day started, with her asking me a question I couldn't answer without talking to Brady first.

"I got here late, and I was tired."

She seemed to mull that over for a while, then nodded. "Dad has a big bed. You should have shared it."

"Uhm… oh… okay." Way to sound like an idiot.

"You're really tall, even when you're laying down. Is that because you ate all your vegetables?"

That was a minefield of a question. If I said yes she might decide she wouldn't eat vegetables so she stayed shorter, if I said no, then she might decide eating vegetables served no practical purpose.

"It's genetics," I winced inwardly. Why did I say that? What I know about genetics is buried in twelfth-grade biology lessons, and it had all gone over my head.

"Okay," she accepted. "I'll get the bagels."

I stood up then, stretched tall and walked my fingers on their ceiling, bones popping, and my back straightening after a night on the couch.

"Hey you," Brady circled my waist from behind, and I turned in his arms. "I tried to wake you, but you were dead to the world. Come with me." He tugged me to the kitchen where Maddie was putting out a collection of jams, along with cream cheese spread, four plates, and knives. "Maddie, Eric is my boyfriend."

She gave what I can only call a duh expression. "I know that."

"He might be staying over sometimes."

"That's good." She brushed it off as a non-event. "Do you like peanut butter, Eric?"

"Of course he does," Lucas said from my side, and even if I didn't like it there was no way I would disagree. I noticed the close hug that Lucas gave Brady, and it seemed to have meaning to it. "Morning, Dad," he said.

Yep, definite meaning. Something had happened here, and I wonder if Brady would tell me.

As readily as that, they'd accepted I was in the house, and they peppered me with questions all day long about being a firefighter, about how I got so tall, about Cap the dog, about the sky, where rain comes from, and blessedly they never once asked me about the fires in the hills. It was a perfect day, quiet, sitting in the beautiful garden, holding hands with Brady, kissing him, talking over the week, and finding my center.

"Are you on call?" he asked as we went to bed. I realized he hadn't asked me that all day, maybe he'd avoided it, so it didn't remind me.

"Not really, but, if I'm needed…"

He hugged me again, then turned on the bedside light. His room had one wall full of sketches and artwork, and I could see the new ones, the scarlet engine and firefighter teddies. He curled into my side, and I wish I wasn't so tired that I could pull him against me and we could make love.

"I'm sorry—"

"Shhhh, sleep."

So I did.

My cell woke me a little before five, and I answered it immediately, aware that Brady sat upright in bed with me.

"They're calling for teams," Dale advised. "I'm texting you the info." My cell chimed with the incoming text. "You have it?" I checked it.

"I have it."

"Is everything okay?" Brady asked, "I know it's not, but I wanted to ask." He looked serious, and I didn't want to leave him worrying, or hell, leave him at all.

"Clean up work," I lied, then kissed him on the forehead. "I love you."

"I love you. Stay safe."

"I can call you later when I'm done?"

He gripped me briefly, and then let me go. "Okay, "Okay."

I made it to Command in the location advised, and everything was eerily quiet. No fire in view, minimal smoke over the ridge, and all senior officers were in a loose circle around the Operation Sections Chief, examining two information boards, the rest of us hanging back.

I didn't have time to think about Brady telling me he loved me, or the night we'd slept in the same bed and hugged, or the strength his quiet understanding and support gave me, I was on duty now, and from the details in the text, the shit had really hit the fan.

"You think we have national resources coming in?" Frankie asked, and I shook my head because I had no freaking idea where we were at. There was a three-tiered system: local, regional, and national when it came to dealing with these forest fires. Local was a 911 call reporting a fire, with the dispatcher sending out local firefighters from the immediate area. If the fire was judged to be more of a risk, then it was pushed to regional. Sometimes the flames grew too quickly, becoming more extensive and more complex than the initial responders could handle. That was when the dispatcher would escalate again.

"GACC has rounded up assistance from Marin County and Big Bear," Dale confirmed as he rejoined us.

"They called in regional support?" I heard Frankie mutter, "Shit, this doesn't sound good."

The unspoken question was whether the regional coordinator had called the national broker for fire resources. If that had happened, then it was past serious and onto deadly. Firefighters from Idaho, Nevada, Oregon,

Wyoming, and Colorado had already reported to the wildfires in Southern California this year, and we'd been glad of their help. Was this fire as big and out of control as the one that had burned the town of Paradise? What were we facing? A weird combination of fear and excitement churned in my belly. This is what we were trained for, but fire was an unpredictable mistress, and we had to fear her as well.

"As yet undetermined," Dale said, which was probably as much as we could hope to hear. Then he led the four of us toward our unit chief who had twenty-five years of fighting fires.

"Fire got away from fifty-nine," he stated, as other teams gathered around him.

"Only because they're on rotated shutdown," Frankie snapped. Saving money was what it was all about. The San Diego fire department was already the country's most underfunded, and rotating brownouts, temporarily closing firehouses to save money, was a disaster waiting to happen. Seconds count, and a lack of support in specific areas left residents vulnerable.

Dale read from his scratched notes. "PG&E has a warning to nine counties that it's considering shutting off power."

Shit, that wasn't good. It was Parker who vocalized what we all wanted to say. "Fuck, nine?"

"So what do we have?" I asked, needing to move away from contemplating what might be happening to actually knowing.

"Three fires sparked out along the highway here, and here," he stabbed at the map, "spotted at fifteen-hundred hours yesterday, a portion of the road was shut down, and firefighters worked overnight to put out the last of the small brush fires. The highway fire was one hundred percent contained at forty-five acres by about 8 a.m. this morning, and we had teams remaining on for most of the morning to mop up the mess," he paused and checked that each us was listening. "These fires were precursors." He let that sink in for a second, more to give himself time to think than to let us question him. "We're out in five on the protection detail for residential areas. Weather is bad, evacuations are underway, and two lanes of the interstate are closed, with a view to more."

He didn't have to say anything else. We got the importance and urgency, and the five of us were focused when we climbed in the engine.

"Our evacuation location is the parking lot at the casino, and the Red Cross is setting up overnight evac at Malone Creek Middle School for those in need."

Those places were so far apart, but when San Diego has hundreds of miles of wildland butted up next to urban spaces, the results could be disastrous. He passed on the critical information from AirTac twenty-nine, the planes spotting for us as they dropped water or fire retardants. What we had here was a perfect storm, heat and dry brush, and the air quality was going to be shit. We finally headed out, following the highway for eleven or so miles, approaching the growing fire from the west, with a southerly breeze pushing the heel of the fire thankfully away from the suburbs of Malone Creek, which had two thousand souls and sat bang in the middle of the worst of the dry areas.

We worked as a well-oiled group, one that had seen a lot of action fighting these fires, and after five minutes of setting up, we were joined by two new teams.

"Emmet Johns, with the CDCR team, starting a twenty-four."

We all acknowledged each other, comrades in fighting this fire. The CDCR team was made up of convicts. With the workforce for CALFIRE depleted, the CDCR provided a workforce. Inmates occupied temporary camps to augment the number of firefighters. I didn't care what a man had done in his past if he was willing to stand by my side and tackle the fire, and that is what most of us thought. I bumped fists with the nearest guys and made myself known to the team leader. We confirmed call signs, organized into groups, had our orders, and all of us drove or walked into hell.

Panic manifests itself in so many ways, when we found people trapped by fire, or threatened, some would run blindly, not caring where or how they were managing to get away, others would stand like deer in headlights, unable to move. It was the latter that was our first shitfest experience of the day. Partnered with Frankie, plus two from the convict team, we were positioned at the end of the fire line, which touched close to a ranch. Frankie indicated clearance, and the four of us headed that way, which is when we found the owner of the ranch, staring at the orange glow of the fire over the ridge and not moving at all.

"We need to get you out of here, sir," Frankie got there first.

"I let them all go," he said, not taking his eyes off the fire. "All of them."

I glanced around, seeing feeding troughs, stables, "Your horses? Sir? Is that what you mean?"

"Some of them ran right to the fire," he pointed up at the ridge. "Why would they do that? I saved them, but they ran…" His hand was shaking. He was clearly in shock. Frankie nudged him to walk, but he wasn't going to step away from where he had a clear view of the direction his horses had run.

"Control, we have a civilian here," I reported. "We need evac."

All I got was static.

"He has a jeep," Frankie pointed at the vehicle which had its nose aimed away from the fire. "Sir, I need you to get in your jeep and go. Head for the casino. Are you with me?"

"But they ran…" He coughed and tears started streaming from his eyes, and then he did the unthinkable, he stepped toward the fire.

"Sir, wait, your horses, we saw them," I said, pulling the lie from a place of wanting to see this guy live.

"You're lying to me," the rancher shouted and lurched forward, out of my reach.

One of the convict fire guys moved in front of him to stop him walking, *Banks* according to the fluorescent letters on his fire coat, one exactly the same as ours. Out there it didn't matter if a man was CALFIRE-employed or one of the convict teams, we were all working toward the same goal. He dropped his equipment to the ground and placed both hands on the rancher's shoulders. I couldn't see much of the convict's face, but his voice was firm and brooked no discussion. "They turned away from the fire, and last we saw they were heading casino way. I promise you they're okay."

The rancher stared, then something in him must have snapped free. I don't remember the heat, or the bruising weight of smoke stealing the oxygen in the air. I don't know how the fire behind us was spreading. That wasn't my job. Right now, this civilian life was vital, and my only focus.

"They need me," he said, coughing and spluttering through the tears.

"Get in the jeep, sir," Banks ordered, and guided the rancher to his jeep, and all four of us watched briefly to ensure he'd left the area. Not that we could've stopped him if he came back. Then it would be part of our job to retrieve his body, after all, we didn't choose this career just to save people, sometimes we were we there to provide closure to loved ones after a death.

"Eric," I introduced myself to Banks, shouting over the growing hissing and spitting of the fire.

"Jason," he called back.

Then there was no time for talking at all. We rejoined the line, but worryingly it wasn't a wall of flame we were behind that was our immediate worry, it was a blizzard of embers, blowing back at us.

"Wind's fucking changed," Frankie shouted, and through the crackling, we got the order to pull back. We retreated as organized as when we'd arrived, making it back to the Command Center, which was buzzing with vehicles.

"Flames angling at forty-five degrees heading down

the canyon," Dale said as he jogged back to us. "We need to get the school evac'd to the casino."

By the time we reached the school, some of the more distant outbuildings were fully involved, embers landing on our jackets, and respiratory protection wasn't just an option.

"The school is evac'd," Frankie called back, but we had to be sure. There wouldn't have been any kids there, but it took no more than a few minutes to check that everyone in the school was gone, evac'd by a quicker team.

By the time we left the school, there were small fires, but the blaze was edging around the property.

There wasn't the panic of other fires, Malone Creek had taken mandatory evacuation to heart, and everything had been cleared before us, so we headed to the casino ten miles west of the fire. We passed crews creating fire breaks, dodged tanker runs, heard the calm but severe nature of every single call.

Evac at the casino was chaos, though. No one had expected the fires to head that way. The casino was safe, hell, we'd sent the rancher there. I saw his jeep, loaded with people, as he drove away fast from the casino to the highway, following whatever plan the chief had laid out.

"We're last on final checks," Dale urged, and the five of us headed directly into the almost empty casino. We got out the last of the staff who were with the injured, the medevac leaving as we did our final checks.

"Radio is fried," Gemma said, frustration in her voice.

"We'll do one last search, and then we're out of here."

The door slammed open, and four men ran in,

barricading the door. "No exit," the first guy said, and I recognized Jason from earlier.

"Eric, Parker, sitrep."

I didn't have to look far—the fire had cut our exit off, tongues of flame rushing our way, behind a snowstorm of embers. It was true that firefighters fight new fires by remembering the past and the things they'd learned. I'd been trapped before, and I was sure it would happen again. That was why we had procedures, because fires don't always start when resources are available, and sometimes you were on your own, or the team was, and actions were based on having no support.

"Well, fuck," Frankie muttered.

We followed protocol, hunkered down, attempted to get hold of Command, but the connection was crackling to non-existent. Not one of us panicked, although there were telltale signs of worry. I saw Frankie and Gemma touch hands, I watched Parker pray, Dale shut his eyes in deep thought, but it was Jason I ended up watching the most.

He met my gaze and quirked a smile. "This turned to shit fast," he said, with that gallows humor that only a person in fear of his life could use.

"Yeah."

"Can't say as I was expecting the day to end like this." His voice had a hint of the south, his words drawled, and his green eyes were bright with emotion, and he slid down the wall to sit on the floor, staring at me, his legs pulled up, calm and composed. He was right. This wasn't how I wanted my day to go, and I wished I could rewind to the last moment with Brady and hold him that bit longer.

Maybe tell him that I loved him over and over until I'd used up all the love I wanted to give him.

"There's clear ground around the casino, deliberately kept that way, and there would have been a clearance of gutters, we're in the best place right now."

He cracked a smile then. "You don't need to reassure me. I know my job."

"I didn't mean to…"

"Shit," he drawled, "I was messing with you. This place here is as good as it gets to sit and wait."

We could hope that the fire bypassed us, or went over us.

"Amen to that," Parker murmured.

Dale's radio crackled and he connected—we couldn't make out much, and he asked them to repeat, over and over.

Finally, the message was more precise.

"Dozer's punched through the fire. We need to evac now." The seven of us didn't hesitate. With the choice of being trapped inside a structure, despite trying to reassure ourselves it was safe, and the possibility of getting away, every one of us made the proactive decision.

The exterior fire door was wedged, and warm to touch, not hot, but enough to know there had been fire the other side. Something in the building had shifted, and buckled the door enough for it to be stuck solid, but between us we had the door wedged open with me taking the weight of it, and Frankie urging people out. Jason was last, shoving Frankie out first.

"I got this," Jason said, as the structure shifted above

us. The door let out a grinding whine of metal on brick, and I shook my head.

"Get out." He hesitated a moment then stepped through, waiting on the other side, helping me away from the door, seconds before it groaned and buckled completely. Then without thought, we sprinted, past the wall of flame which threatened us with scarlet and orange. The dozer was moving away, the last of the others scrambling into the vehicle behind. We weren't going to make it, yards between the two of us as we sprinted in our heavy gear, the terror of dying giving us wings. Something exploded to our left, the acrid searing burn of pine, and Jason stumbled over a nest of discarded branches. He was slightly ahead of me. I caught him to steady him, but he fell, I fell, and a branch pierced my leg as I twisted severely. Jason scrambled to stand, but I was stuck, my leg at an odd angle, the branch jagged and deep in my skin. I couldn't put weight on my leg at all.

He stared at me in horror, then at the fire, and without hesitation, he ripped open my shelter and then did the same for himself. He dragged and cursed, me and the branch in my leg, back to a pre-burned slice of earth, then yanked me down, grabbed me so hard I fell forward in pain.

"Run," I shouted over the flames.

"Fuck that," Jason snarled, both of us knowing death was only seconds behind us. Then in a smooth and practiced move, Jason pulled the shelters over both of us as best he could and we lay still as Hell burned around us.

TWENTY-TWO

Brady

"There's been an accident."

I knew for a fact that Sean was standing at my door telling me something awful. The sky was cerulean blue, cloudless, the manzanita by my drive had attracted a hummingbird, and it was darting about so fast I couldn't focus on it correctly. I knew I had coffee, or at least, I'd been holding coffee, but my hands were empty. My pulse raced, my heart beating overtime, hammering. All I could think was that maybe it was better not to love anyone than to love and have someone taken from you.

It's wrong to plan for a future. Bad things happen, no matter what I do.

Someone was talking to me, shaking me, my whole world spinning.

"He's okay, Brady, look at me. Eric's okay."

I heard Maddie's voice, calling for Uncle Spencer, and I felt her hold my hand and snuggle into my side. I was on the couch, and somehow I'd moved there, but I don't recall how. Then I heard Spencer's voice, and that was when everything became real.

"Fire changed direction... trapped... left behind... hospital."

I stood, willed myself to calm the hell down, and settled my breathing.

"Where is he?" I asked.

"I'll take you," Sean ushered me to the door.

"Lucas and Maddie—"

"I'll stay here with them," Spencer said, and I saw Lucas hugging Maddie close and that she was crying. Fear gripped me, and I yanked at Sean to stop him walking.

"Is he dead?"

Sean cupped my elbows and met my gaze then repeated everything I am sure he'd already said once. "He had to have an operation, a branch pierced his thigh, but he was the lucky one. He's sleeping now, but he's going to be fine." There was an absolute conviction in Sean's voice, and I believed everything was okay. "It could have been worse," he added, and I didn't want to hear that, because I knew what that meant. It didn't mean he was okay, just that he was wasn't dead. We drove to the hospital in silence, but that was more because of me than Sean, in fact, he tried to start a couple of conversations about how everything was going to be okay.

When we arrived, the first person I saw was Leo and arranged behind him familiar faces from the barbecue, and some I didn't know.

"Dale Radford," one of the strangers said. "Eric is part of my team." We shook hands, but I didn't want to talk to

Dale, I wanted to see Eric, I needed to know Sean wasn't lying to me.

"Can I see Eric?" I blurted, talking all over Eric's boss. "Is that even allowed? I'm not family."

"He asked to see you," Sean encouraged, and together we headed down a long corridor, stopping by a glass door into a room with Eric in bed hooked up to equipment with wires and tubes. In the middle of it all, big, strong, but pale and unmoving, lay Eric.

"How did he ask for me? He's not even awake."

"When he arrived at the hospital, they called me, he was asking to see you before they operated, but—"

"What did they do? What happened?" Sean was a doctor—he would know. "Was he awake? Is he burned? Will he wake up again?" I moved to the bed and searched for a hand to hold, then leaned over and kissed Eric's forehead.

There was a flurry of commotion at the door. "Talk to us, Sean," Leo said. "What happened?"

I wanted to shout *me first!* But these were Eric's closest friends, and I faltered in my conviction that I even deserved to be here.

Eric loves me. He thinks I'm strong.

There was fear in this room, Leo was red in the face and breathing heavily. He must have run up here, Sean was pale and nervous, and the room smelled of smoke.

"Tell me," I pleaded.

"He was running from the fire, and he fell and impaled himself on a branch, then…" Sean paused, and I wanted to scream, "… he and another firefighter had to employ their fire shelters and let the fire do its worst."

"Fuck," Leo cursed with feeling and sat down. "What about the other firefighter?"

Sean shook his head, "Third-degree burns to his right side, at least he's stable."

Eric was unconscious, his leg wrapped up, pale. "How did it happen?" I interjected, not comprehending the situation. *How did the man I love get hurt?*

"I don't know." Sean was honest at least, and he sat and rested his arms on his elbows until it was only me standing by the bed—there was no way I was leaving Eric's side. I was determined that one of the first people he saw when he woke was me.

How long we waited I didn't know, but when he first stirred, Sean was at one side, and I was the other, but he wasn't focused enough to look at either of us. It took a while for him to be completely present in the room, but Sean called in the doctor, who announced that the surgery had been clean and that there might not be any lasting damage. He used the word *lucky* again, and after he left, Sean did some checks of his own, making small noises of approval at all the readings on the chart.

"You're an idiot, Eric," Leo's voice was gruff as he squeezed Eric's shoulder, "and lazy."

"Fuck you, Five-Oh," Eric sounded shaky, but he half-smiled.

"We're leaving you in Brady's hands," Sean said, and ruffled Eric's hair, and began to leave.

"Wait, what about Jason, the guy I was with?"

Sean closed his eyes, then sighed. "He'll be okay," he summarized.

"He saved my life. Find out what's happening, look after him."

"We're on it," Leo said, and then it was just Eric and me in the room. Eric gripped my hand and wriggled a little before wincing. There were muffled creaks as Eric tried to get comfortable in bed, then he stopped moving as if he couldn't find that spot where he wouldn't hurt.

"Everything's okay," he said, comforting me as if I was the one who needed to be reassured.

"Fuck," I cursed with feeling. "That's my line." I offered him some ice chips, and when I leaned over, I pressed a hard kiss to his forehead, the scent of smoke stronger on his skin. The idea of him trapped in a fire, of being hurt filled my thoughts. Was it possible to be in love with someone who could be taken from me at any moment? He made me feel like a better man, stronger, but if I lost him, would I ever fall in love again? I'd lost my sister, my parents, what else could I lose? I would isolate myself with the children, become something even I didn't recognize.

"Stop overthinking," Eric insisted, and reached for me, tugging me closer. I buried my face against his neck and tears pricked my eyes, emotion closing my throat.

"I love you," I whispered.

I felt the chuckle, the rumble in his chest, and then the words he passed back to me, which meant everything. "I love you, too."

"Eric?" I turned to see a woman in the doorway, petite, pearls, like a tiny Jackie-O and behind her a distinguished older man. The woman went straight to Eric, kissed him on the forehead, and she was crying. The man was stoic at first, but as soon as he got a real look at Eric in the bed, I could see the façade crumble.

"Mom, Dad," Eric said, and I moved back to allow them their time. Someone else lurked in the doorway, a big guy, maybe even bigger than Eric, he wore an earpiece, and the bulge in his jacket implied a gun.

"What happened, son?" the man asked, but Eric couldn't answer, in fact, I was surprised he was even awake with the anesthetic barely worn off and the pain meds in action.

Eric's dad straightened after pressing his own kiss to Eric's hair, then he and the woman hugged and exchanged whispers. I felt like a voyeur and began to veer carefully toward the door, but the bodyguard stopped my exit. Ordinarily, I might have panicked at being cornered, but Eric's room had a wall of glass, and I had to be able to trust his family. Right?

Instead of leaving, I leaned back on the glass and thought about my breathing and how I was going to recall this moment even if it killed me. Then his dad turned to face me and extended a hand, which I shook. "David Lester-Hythe," he announced, "and this is Polly."

"You must be Brady!" Polly exclaimed.

Eric mumbled something which sounded a lot like, "Mom, Dad, leave Brady alone." But Polly was hugging me into her perfumed embrace and held me before stepping back. She cupped my shoulders, and her eyes were wet with tears.

"It's so wonderful to meet you finally. Eric has told us all about you," she said and stepped away. I could see Eric in the size of his dad, but it was his mom's smile that he'd inherited. They visited for ten minutes or so, Polly not letting go of Eric's hand for a single minute after she'd let go of me. David, on the other hand, took one of the chairs and watched Eric with affectionate eyes, letting his wife do all the talking. Eric himself was quiet, dozing on and off, and I was just about to make my excuses so they could have alone time when the bodyguard stepped fully into the room.

"Senator, the car is here," Mr. Bodyguard said.

Polly hugged me again, and this time she had tears in her eyes. "I'm so pleased that Eric has someone special, you must bring the children to the house to visit. I would love to get to know you better."

"Thank you. I will." I was dazed and a little disoriented as we said our goodbyes, and then thankfully it was just Eric and me again.

"Your mom and dad are awesome," I half-asked for confirmation.

"Hmmm," Eric said, and then fell asleep.

Compassion and fear swamped me, and I touched his hand gently. "I love you so much, even if your parents have a bodyguard and you're probably rich as Croesus, asshole."

By day two Eric was grumpy, he hated being stuck in bed, and he wanted to visit with Jason, the firefighter who'd saved his life, and who was in a room a few doors down. Only Jason hadn't been allowed random visitors, not because he was too injured, but because he was a convict from one of the convict volunteer teams. I hadn't even seen any of his family and they would have had to get past Eric's room to reach Jason.

I suggested that I take a message, which was rash, because that meant recalling the message, evading the nurses, and the odd marauding doctor, and bypassing security. The latter was fine, if I timed it right. I was cleared to be on this floor, and the security for his room was based at the desk by the door to this corridor. If I seemed confident enough and didn't fall over, I could probably pull it off.

Jason was awake, the TV in the corner playing an infomercial for a floor mop which was allegedly going to change the lives of every American. He wasn't watching it. Instead, he was staring out the window, and I don't think he even heard me come in.

"Hi," I said, and he slowly turned to face me. With dark hair and bright blue eyes, he didn't appear very old. Maybe early twenties, and he was not only covered in bandages, but his face was bruised.

"Hi," he said back, and his voice sounded like gravel, as he coughed, and then winced.

"Don't move; it's okay. My name is Brady."

"Jason," he whispered back at me.

I stepped closer to the bed and got a better look at him.

"Thank you for saving Eric. I owe you everything for what you did." He blinked up at me as if he didn't understand, and then in a moment or two, his eyes widened. "I'm Eric's boyfriend, and you saved the man I love. If there is anything I can do for you, *we* can do for you. You only have to ask. Thank you." I wasn't entirely sure what I could've done to help him, but maybe Eric would be able to do something when he was up and out of bed.

"Is he okay?" Jason coughed again.

I gripped his hand. "Thanks to you, I know what you did, how you covered him, how you stopped to help him, I've never heard anything so brave before." He tightened his fingers briefly, and then shut his eyes, and I think he was done talking. One more squeeze and I left, making it back to Eric with seconds to spare as security walked by to check. I don't know what kind of convict Jason was, but security wasn't on the level of cops with guns. I'd have to ask Leo.

"Is he okay?" Eric asked. "What did you say?"

I kissed Eric, then pulled back a little. "I told him I owed him for saving your life, and he asked after you. He'll be okay, Eric."

"I'll ask my dad to... he should..." he coughed again.

"Sleep, Eric, I'll be here when you wake up."

Eric slept for a while, but by the end of the day, he wanted to go home.

Day three was messy. I can't even think about how lousy day three was, but at least Eric got to visit with Jason, and they spent a good hour talking on their own. When Eric's parents arrived, I left them to it and took a cab home to check in with Maddie and Lucas. I'd been back to the house each night, but today being Saturday, I was collecting them to take them back to the hospital with me. When they arrived at Eric's room, they didn't care that there was a huge ass bodyguard in the doorway, or that Eric had visitors. They rushed over, and Maddie hugged him hard, with Lucas asking questions about the fire. It was Polly who got all kinds of information out of Lucas and Maddie about everything from their favorite colors to their wishes and hopes for the future. Maddie fell for Eric's mom immediately, sitting next to her and chatting at length about kittens and puppies, of all things.

David was definitely a politician because he had Lucas eating out of his palm in less than ten minutes flat, asking for Lucas' opinion on all kinds of things. The icing on the cake was when he wondered if Lucas could help him set up Instagram, which Lucas loved. Through all of this, I sat on the edge of Eric's bed and held his hand, and for a lot of it, he went from sleeping to irritable.

I think the visit tired Eric, or maybe it was that he didn't want to answer questions about the fire, either way, he was crabby and pissed and wanted to go home. Only it didn't stop him from asking his dad to set in motion an examination into Jason's term in jail, which David said he'd already begun. None of us actually knew what Jason had done in the past, but he'd saved Eric's life, and we would always owe him.

Thankfully, on day four, Eric was allowed home, with instructions to attend PT and to take his meds. Sean wheeled him from the hospital, and when we reached the parking area, I began my goodbyes to Eric, explaining how I would visit as often as I could, and that I would miss him. We made it to the car before Eric interrupted me, poking my belly with a finger.

"I thought I'd come to your place to recover, keep you company, sit in the garden, that kind of thing."

"Oh," I managed, and for a moment his expression of hope dimmed.

"If that was okay," he said.

I didn't really have to think long. "Yeah, I'd like that."

Something passed between him and Sean, but Sean smiled, and they fist-bumped—it seemed as if everything was settled. Eric, the man I loved, was recuperating at my house and Maddie and Lucas would be in their element.

Having Eric around was good for me. When Brooke called me about running workshops at the college, he talked me into doing it. He was in my face all the time, making me laugh, pulling me from my shell, complimenting my art, making coffee, and it was as if we'd lived together forever. The days were quiet for him, but we found ways around his injury to make love, although it was gentler lovemaking, a stronger connection that had my thoughts all over the place.

The more he talked to me about what I *could* do, the more I believed in myself, and something big inside me clicked and slid into place. I *was* a strong man, and I just needed to stop thinking I wasn't. He showed me that I was stronger than I thought, both in his silent approval and his forceful demands that I go out and beat life. I wasn't ever going to be the guy who lit up the world, my sensory issues, my overwhelming need for peace, were all at war with modern living, but whatever, I loved him for what he was doing.

And it culminated in the fact that today was a big day.

Today is the first day of the rest of my life.

Of our *lives.*

I was starting at college, and he was going back to work. Eric packed a lunch for me to take to my first day of actually going into college, just as he'd been doing for the kids. He was due back at the firehouse today, not on active duty yet, but in the office. I was trying my absolute hardest not to worry about him, but I guess falling in love with a first responder meant I'd have to face that fear every day.

I wasn't due into the art center until ten, and after Maddie and Lucas went to school, I had at least an hour to get myself ready and go to college which involved one final pep talk from Eric who wished he could drive me. I ordered a cab and spent the last ten minutes I had at home kissing Eric. Not a bad way to spend a short amount of time.

I made my way through the campus, with careful, measured steps, my shiny new security card around my neck, ignoring the press of college kids who all seemed to be in a hurry to get somewhere. I found the building I needed, took the stairs to the third floor and, shoulders back, I headed to the last door on the left. The corridor seemed to go on forever, like Alice in Wonderland I felt the walls close in to a pinpoint. I stopped for a while and rummaged in my bag to cover the fact I was standing there with my eyes closed, focusing on my breathing.

I could do this on my own. I was in college. Not like school remedial classes, not where I would receive pity assignments with coloring options from teachers who wished I was in a special ed group. This was real learning, and I was ready.

I think I'm ready.

I got as far as the door, I even had my hand on the handle, before the sickness washed over me. I was hot, my heart beat loudly, and my vision tunneled to a pinpoint of light in a sea of blurry grey.

"I've got it, dude," a young man said next to me, as he opened the door.

"Thank you," I think I said, but it may well have been a grunt for all I knew.

With a hand at the small of my back, he ushered me in and closed the door, and I blinked away the gray. This place wasn't like the school I recalled. There weren't any tables in rows, but a big square of them. Where was I supposed to stand? In my head, I'd been at the front of the room with a whiteboard explaining my theories, drawing, and not having to look or talk to anyone.

That wasn't what I saw at all. The guy took a seat at the far side, immediately entering into a conversation with a cute blonde who hung on his every word, bobbing her head at him and grinning. No one stared at me or pointed at me, so that was a start, but I knew I had to choose somewhere to sit and put my things. No teacher's table, not that I was teaching, but still, what the hell was I doing here?

"Are you the artist?" the blonde asked me, and I jerked in surprise, lost in my thoughts.

"I am, yes."

"Cool, you drew the Mu 7 stuff, right?"

That was what I was known for I guess, a graphic sci-fi novel with gay protagonists that had moderate success in a specific demographic. I nodded and took the few steps to the nearest desk, dropping my bag and taking a seat before I did something stupid like fall over a chair.

"I love Mu 7," she announced and I saw the boy sitting next to her nod in agreement. "So does my girlfriend."

"Thank you." I wasn't expecting more, but she launched into a comparison between my work and other graphic novels she'd bought, and before I knew it I felt more relaxed and answered a few of her questions. By the time it was ten, there were five people in the room, four students and me. Two boys, two girls, spread out around the boxed tables and all looking at me expectantly. Where did I start? I pulled out my notes and placed them in front of me.

I want to leave.

Summarize the aims of this project.

No. I really want to go.

It's only for six weeks. This is good for you.

I could leave, it's not like anyone is paying me, I don't owe anything to anyone.

"Sir? Mr. McMillan? I had an idea."

The blonde was waving her arm, and the three others groaned good-naturedly. It seemed as if she was the one full of ideas, and that would be a great way to start. Forget me doing a long rambling explanation; they all knew why they were in the room, and they didn't need me to lecture them. I was facilitating, that was all.

"Okay, how about we introduce ourselves and talk a bit about what ideas we might have." I gestured to the blonde to go first.

"I'm Alicia," the blonde with the ideas said. "I've been working on this edgy cross between a kind of *Star Wars* vibe and *Alien,* but with a nod to *As the World Turns*." She sat back in her seat, looking very happy with herself, but all I could focus on was that she wanted to create something edgy that gave the nod to a daytime soap?

"Cool," I said and glanced at the boy next to her.

"I'm Louis, like Tomlinson, you know? And I love

your Mu 7 stuff," he said, and that seemed to be the extent of his idea range.

"I'm Colin, and I was thinking..." Colin, a red-headed kid with a nose ring seemed shy. "You know how in 1978, Will Eisner's *A Contract with Go*d was formatted with sepia-tone pages, and that it had four semi-biographical stories about a Bronx tenement and its inhabitants in the 1930s..."

The other three groaned, and he went scarlet.

"Carry on," I encouraged. I don't think the others meant to embarrass him, or at least I hope they didn't. He knew his stuff, the same things I knew and loved, the geek in me happy to hear other people liked what I did, and I wanted to listen to what he had to say.

"How about the uhmm... four of us, doing separate stories, but linking them."

"What would your story be about?" Alicia asked.

"I was thinking a story grounded in the modern-day—"

"That wouldn't fit in with my story," Alicia pointed out. "What do you—?"

"I'm Sue," the last student interrupted. She side-eyed Colin, who was still scarlet. "And I love Colin's idea."

If anything Colin got redder, but it was nice to see someone sticking up for him. I knew what it was like to have someone take the time to listen to me and support me, and how loved I felt when it happened. I couldn't stop thinking about Lucas, Maddie, and Eric, and every time I felt overwhelmed, it was their faces I focused on. They loved that I was so determined, and I owed it to myself to stay calm and in control.

I can do this.

"Okay then, this is how we start. I need you to sketch a character for me, think of a theme, pass it to each other, workshop the ideas, and I'll be here to talk and assist, and hopefully, by the end of today, we will have a workable idea. It could be a soap opera in space with the theme of redemption or a sepia-toned slice of reality that focuses on mental health. Whatever it is that you have as a vision, try and get it down on paper and that will give us somewhere to start. Does that seem okay to everyone?" That was possibly the longest sentence I'd spoken in years, and my chest felt tight with the weird breathing I had going on as I talked.

They all nodded, pulling out sketch pads, and cell phones, pens, Colin even had paint, and heads down, they spent the first half-hour concentrating on their work. I sat for a while with each of them. Colin was meticulous in his drawing, Sue seemed lost in her focus, but her drawing was rounded and lovely to look at. Louis was all about warfare and robots, and Alicia had somehow managed to encapsulate *Star Wars*, *Alien*, and soap operas into four sections on her page.

I just knew this short-term project was going to be interesting.

And when I got home, it was Taco-Friday, and the four of us made the most awesome tacos known to man. Or at least that's what Eric said.

When the kids were in bed, we had some alone time, sitting on the patio in the warm evening air.

"How was your day back at work?" I asked, because he hadn't volunteered the information, and I got the sense he didn't want to talk about it in front of Maddie and Lucas.

Instead, he'd focused entirely on me and how my day had been. He paused before answering, and I wonder if that was because he thought I wouldn't want to hear. "You can tell me. I bet it was exciting."

"Frustrating. Wonderful. I ache. But it's good to be back. Thought about you all day."

I'd fallen in love with the bravest of men, and I couldn't have been happier.

Epilogue

ERIC

THE ENGINE GLEAMED.

I'd put hours into making the paintwork shine, every part of it was like silk to the touch, and when I stood back to admire it, I felt so much pride it hurt. Tomorrow was my first day back on active duty, but today was all about rewarding bravery.

"He's here," Frankie announced, and I followed him out to greet Jason. He was accompanied by security, but to look at him, I wouldn't have known he was a prisoner and had another six months to serve on his sentence. We hugged, we'd gone past shaking hands after what we'd been through together, and if he hadn't saved me, I wouldn't have been polishing the damn truck ready to get to work. We didn't have much chance to talk before he was whisked away by the guard and the Chief. Mom and Dad were there as well, so this whole event had become a big thing. Jason was a hero, but it didn't appear as if he was happy with the intense scrutiny. He was on edge, and I was waiting for him to ask to be taken back to the convict conservation camp.

Leo sidled up to me and tugged me away from the family. "So I checked Jason out as you asked," Leo murmured. Dad had refused to tell me details, so Leo was my last attempt to help Jason out. Dad had said that Jason was refusing help, and planned to serve the remainder of his sentence in peace for reasons he didn't tell us and that even as a Senator, he couldn't do anymore.

"And?"

"White-collar stuff, not a federal crime, plea bargain, blah, blah."

"Can we do anything about it?" I asked immediately.

"Like what?"

I huffed. "He's not a bad guy, Leo. He's one of the good ones."

Eric raised an eyebrow. "Jason pleaded guilty," he pointed out, then sighed, "but yeah, I'm trying to do my thing, okay?"

"Thanks."

"In return, I need you to explain to Mia that my name is not Five-oh."

I attempted to look serious and understanding. "Of course," I lied. There was no way I was letting that long-running plan come to a stop any time soon, particularly since Mia was still confusing Five-oh with Fido, which was funny as shit.

We assembled in the bay, a journalist from the local paper at the edge, chatting on his phone, which was kind of disrespectful so he'd better get off it fast. Then I spotted

Sean and beyond him Brady, Lucas, and Maddie. As soon as she spotted me, she darted my way, and I caught her as she flew into my arms. I'd moved into their home when I'd left the hospital, and six months later, I hadn't left. Poor Leo had the entire house to himself now, even though Sean and I had an investment in it still. We weren't pulling out, but Leo had been making noises about taking in lodgers, maybe from his station. I missed him and Sean, they missed me, but that didn't stop any of us meeting up at the old house and sitting in the chairs at the bottom of the yard, and of course, we still met up to do volunteer work at the kids' home.

I'd settled in with Brady as if I was supposed to be there. I was the one who helped the kids with math and English, Brady covered the arts, we both went to the most recent parents' evening and held hands the entire time, and we did the grocery shopping together. I drove, but it was Brady who planned meals, and we both cooked. He worked in his garden, I studied for exams to make Lieutenant in the future, and through all of it, we fell into bed at the end of each day and enjoyed being in love.

Brady and I sat next to each other, at the end of the row of chairs, because I knew he didn't like being hemmed in. Maddie sat on my other side because she wanted to lean on me, and Lucas listened raptly as our Chief explained what happened the day of the fire and what Jason had done.

"You okay?" Brady asked, for what was probably the tenth time today.

"Yeah," I replied and bumped shoulders with him.

"Love you, big guy," he said and smiled across at me.

"Love you more."

Lucas was going camping this weekend with Cameron,

Maddie was at a sleepover for another one of her house parties, and Saturday night we had the house to ourselves. The ring in my pocket was burning a hole, and who knows, a Saturday without the children, maybe in the garden with the scent of flowers and the warmth of a San Diego evening, I could go down on one knee and propose.

I was absolutely convinced Brady would say yes.

And he did.

THE END

Meet RJ Scott

RJ is the author of the over one hundred published novels and discovered romance in books at a very young age. She realized that if there wasn't romance on the page, she could create it in her head, and is a lifelong writer.

She lives and works out of her home in the beautiful English countryside, spends her spare time reading, watching films, and enjoying time with her family.

The last time she had a week's break from writing she didn't like it one little bit and has yet to meet a bottle of wine she couldn't defeat.

www.rjscott.co.uk | rj@rjscott.co.uk

NEWSLETTER

- facebook.com/author.rjscott
- twitter.com/Rjscott_author
- instagram.com/rjscott_author
- bookbub.com/authors/rj-scott
- pinterest.com/rjscottauthor

Manufactured by Amazon.ca
Bolton, ON